Petal Pushers

Best Buds

Read all the Petal Pushers books!

Too Many Blooms

Flower Feud

Best Buds

Coming Up Roses

Petal Pushers

Best Buds

Catherine R. Daly

SCHOLASTIC INC.

New York   Toronto   London   Auckland

Sydney   Mexico City   New Delhi   Hong Kong

*To Barbara and George for all their encouragement—
especially for the creative writing lessons at
Queens College, way back when.*

With special thanks to Tim Hall for the totally perfect title.

*And a debt of gratitude to James Albertelli of Gramercy
Park Flower Shop for sharing his wealth
of floral knowledge with me.*

❀   ❀   ❀

ISBN 978-0-545-21452-0

12 11 10 9 8 7 6 5 4 3 2 1   9 10 11 12 13 14/0

Printed in the U.S.A. 40
First edition, June 2011

Book design by Yaffa Jaskoll

Chapter One

Last day of school. Are there four sweeter words in the English language?

Not that I dislike school, don't get me wrong. But after conquering seventh grade — four As and one A-minus, thank you very much — I was ready for two whole beautiful months with no homework, essays, or pop quizzes, that was for sure.

I gazed around the cafeteria, where I was sitting at my usual table, finishing up lunch with my friends. The lunchroom was louder than normal, buzzing with a slightly wacky last-day-of-school energy. A group of sixth-grade boys were tossing their milk cartons into a garbage can halfway across the room. Everyone laughed when Eddie Noonan missed and beaned Maria Gonzalez in the head.

She threw it back at him, nailing him right in the stomach. The room erupted into cheers.

"They're going to get detention," said my friend Amy Arthur worriedly, pushing her black, rectangular glasses higher up on the bridge of her nose. Back in fifth grade, a substitute teacher had unjustly accused Amy of passing notes. She'd received her one and only detention and now lived in fear of it — for anyone.

"There's no such thing as detention on the last day of school," our other friend Heather Hanson scoffed, tossing her dirty-blonde corkscrew curls over her shoulder. Heather may look like a china doll, but she is tough as nails. She pointed to a group of teachers, allegedly on lunchroom duty. They were chatting away, oblivious to the cafeteria Olympics. "The teachers want out of here as much as we do."

Amy shrugged and changed the subject. "Are you guys aware that this is the last lunch we will ever have together as seventh graders?" she asked, gazing at each of us solemnly.

"Wow," Jessica Wu said in her sweetly spacey way. Her straight black hair, up in a ponytail, was even spikier than usual. "That's intense!"

"Well, think of it this way," said Becky Davis. "We have a whole year full of eighth-grade lunches to look forward to." Becky tends to look on the bright side of things. (I'm a bit of a pessimist sometimes, so Becky's attitude can be both frustrating *and* refreshing.) She's tall and pretty, with shoulder-length black curls, deep brown eyes, and dark skin. She's the kind of person you'd be totally jealous of if she weren't your BFF. Luckily, she's mine.

I pushed my wavy, light brown hair out of my eyes and glanced down at the time on my cell phone. Ten minutes till the end of lunch. I wondered what my friends were waiting for. If they were planning to surprise me with cake and presents now, they had better hurry up.

Sure, my birthday was more than two weeks away. But this was the last time we were all going to be in one place together till the end of August. It was time to get cracking.

"So when do you leave for Hawaii?" I asked Jessica, knowing full well what the answer was. Maybe they just needed a little reminder. . . .

"Tomorrow morning!" she crowed.

Everyone gazed at her enviously for a moment. Jessica

and her brother were going to spend the entire summer visiting their grandparents, who lived on the island of Maui. Hanging out on pink sand beaches, snorkeling, surfing, the works! Definitely a nice change from our small town of Elwood Falls, New Hampshire.

My friends and I all had different plans for the summer. Becky was leaving for sleepaway tennis camp in a couple of days, and I was missing her already. Heather would spend the month of July in the place her family rented every year in South Carolina. And Amy, whose parents were both elementary school teachers, was going on a cross-country trip in a rented Winnebago. It had an educational bent, which Amy was not all that thrilled about. "But it ends up in Disneyland," she had told us. "So I guess I can't complain. Too much."

I was going away with my family, too, but only for two weeks. Still, I was really excited about our trip. Maine, which borders New Hampshire, is one of my favorite places in the world. Eating lobster rolls and whoopie pies, swimming, clamming, stargazing, catching fireflies, toasting marshmallows for s'mores, picking fresh blueberries for pies and crumbles. What's not to like? We were renting

4

this cool old house by the ocean. And the best part is that my loud, messy, overwhelming family doesn't even bother me so much when we're away. Being the one organized person in a family of six isn't easy. But when we're on vacation none of it seems to matter.

Becky began to gather up the remnants of her lunch into a brown paper bag. "Del, when do you leave for Maine again?" she asked me.

I smiled. Here was my opening. "Friday, July sixth," I said.

No reaction.

"The day before my birthday," I added.

The four stricken faces that looked back at me told me all I needed to know. There would be no birthday party in the lunchroom for me today.

Becky groaned. "That's right!" she cried.

"We should have celebrated today!" said Amy.

Heather grimaced. "Oh, Del, I guess we got all caught up in the last day of school and . . ."

"Totally forgot all about your birthday," finished Jessica. The three other girls gave her a dirty look for stating the obvious.

"What?" she said defensively. "That's what we did!"

I stood up and grabbed my books, fighting down my disappointment. "No big deal," I said.

"I feel awful," said Becky, standing up to give me a hug.

I shrugged. "Really, it's no big deal," I repeated.

But actually, it kind of was. I hate having a summer birthday. I've never had cupcakes in the classroom, the whole class singing "Happy Birthday" to me. My mom always tells me that someday I'll be happy when I'm grown up and I can take myself on a fancy birthday vacation with my friends. But that's all good and fine when I'm, like, thirty.

And I knew I would have fun, celebrating on my actual birthday with my family up in Maine. But just once I'd like to have my friends around to help me celebrate. Unfortunately, they're always on vacation. And for some reason, this year seemed worse than usual. I guess it was because I was about to turn thirteen. You know, the first birthday as a teenager and all that. You were supposed to do something special. Jessica was the first of our group to turn thirteen, back in February. Always up for something different, she had taken us to a roller derby match — the Queen City Cherry Bombs vs. the Elm City Derby Damez. It was awesome. Amy had turned thirteen in March and had had a big bat mitzvah at a fancy catering hall, complete with a DJ and karaoke machine. Heather and Becky wouldn't turn thirteen till October and November, respectively. But they both had big plans.

And then there was me, Del Bloom. Birth date: July 7. Birthstone: Ruby. Sign: Cancer. Flower: Larkspur. Best birthday gift: My dog, Buster, when I was six. Best birthday party: None. No doubt about it, summer birthdays bite.

The bell for the end of lunch rang. I flipped open the front cover of one of the five yearbooks on the table to make sure it was mine. *Dear Del,* I read, *Have a muy excelente summer! Remember all the fun we had in Spanish class. Tu amigo, Jorge.* I clutched the yearbook to my chest and followed my friends out of the cafeteria.

That afternoon, "classes" were a blur of yearbook signing, chatting teachers, and discussing summer plans. Finally, the last bell rang and we surged out of our seats toward the door. Kids started cheering as we spilled into the hallways. Summer vacation had officially begun.

I walked to my locker to pick up my few remaining belongings. I quickly spun the dial around and snapped the lock open. I smiled as I removed the lock and placed it in my backpack. Wouldn't be needing that again till September! I would have the same locker again in the fall, so nothing to be nostalgic about there. I took out my notebooks and folders and slammed my locker shut with finality.

Birthday disappointment aside, it had been a pretty good year. The only glitch had been my grandparents' announcement, back in the spring, that they were moving to Florida — and leaving the family flower shop in my parents' hands. That had been a huge, unwanted surprise. I'd had trouble getting used to the idea of my family running the store that had once, in my mind, just belonged to me and my grandparents. But I had learned to adjust, and things were going pretty well. We had even changed the name from the sort of unwieldy and old-fashioned "Flowers on Fairfield" to the cute and snappy "Petal Pushers."

I turned around to head outside and meet up with my friends when I spotted Carmine Belloni across the hallway. He was leaning against his locker, studying a rectangular piece of paper. I headed over to say good-bye. I was the only girl who had been invited to Carmine's kindergarten birthday party and I still had a soft spot for him because of it. He was just as nice now as he'd been back then.

Carmine looked up. "Hey, Del," he said. "Are you going to the party, too? It's at that new catering place that's supposed to be really cool."

"What party?" I asked, interested. The new catering place sounded super posh, with chandeliers and fountains and marble staircases and all that stuff. Was someone having an end-of-year party? That would be fun!

Carmine held up the piece of paper he had been looking at. I leaned over to take a look. It was a fancy invitation. Gilt letters spelled out ASHLEY'S THIRTEENTH BIRTHDAY.

Ohhhhhh, I thought, instantly understanding why I hadn't received one. "Ashley and I aren't exactly best buds," I explained to him.

"Oh, sorry, Del," he said.

"No problem," I said with a shrug. But I couldn't take my eyes off the thick, cream-colored invite. The gold letters were raised. It looked like an engraved wedding invitation. And then I nearly gasped when I saw the date — July 7.

I couldn't even get four friends together, and Ashley Edwards was going to have a huge party! Not on her actual birthday, which is in mid-July, may I add.

On *mine*.

I finally tore my eyes off the invite. With as much dignity as I could muster I said, "Have fun at the party, Carmine." I told him that I would see him around and headed down the hall.

Where I saw Ashley and her two bodyguards (all right, her best friends) Rachel Lebowitz and Sabrina Jones, deep in conversation.

Maybe I can get by without being seen, I thought. *That would be a nice way to end the school year.* But no such luck.

"Well, hello, Delphinium," Ashley said. She and her two goons stepped in front of me, stopping me in my tracks. I noticed that Rachel and Sabrina were each holding a small stack of cream-colored envelopes in their hands reverentially, as if they were made of pure gold.

I gave Ashley a dirty look. True, Delphinium *is* my

given name. The girls on my mom's side of the family all have flower names. We have an Iris (my gran), a Lily (my great-aunt), a Daisy (my mom), a Rose (my younger sister), an Aster (my other younger sister, and Rose's twin), a Poppy (my littlest sister) and yes, a . . . *Delphinium*. A delphinium is a very pretty purplish blue flower, but it's definitely a difficult name. For the most part, I prefer to be called Del. Ashley, who used to be my best friend back in preschool until we had a falling out, knows this and therefore calls me by my full name all the time. Just to annoy me. That's the kind of person she is.

"Hello, Ashley," I said. I nodded to her friends, who have such similar looks it is hard to tell them apart sometimes. "Rachel, Sabrina," I said to them both. I moved to walk past them, but they blocked my way. Frustrated, I turned to Ashley. She had layered two expensive-looking tank tops over each other, looped a thin dark brown belt around her waist, and wore a handkerchief hem skirt and delicate sandals. I glanced down at my white capri pants, colorful Vans, and tie-dyed T-shirt. I had thought my outfit was stylish when I had looked at myself in the mirror that morning. I shook my head. Fashion-wise, there was just no competing with Ashley,

"Well, this is awk," said Ashley. She loves to talk in shorthand. Why use a full recognizable word when a confusing abbreviation will do? I find it totally ridic, to be honest.

I gave her a puzzled look.

"Me with a stack of invites." She gave me a fake sympathetic smile. "And none for you."

"Oh, are you having a party?" I asked, playing dumb.

"Of course," she said rolling her eyes. "It's my thirteenth." She gave me a condescending smile. "And what are you doing for *your* birthday?" she asked.

"I'm going on vacation," I told her, though it bothered me that I felt like I had to explain anything to her.

"Europe?" asked Ashley. "That's where I went for my twelfth. Paris is lovely this time of year."

I lifted my chin proudly. "No, Maine," I said. Sabrina and Rachel snickered.

Ashley raised her eyebrows. "Interesting choice," she replied, making it perfectly clear that there was absolutely nothing interesting about it at all. Then she turned to her friends. "Let's go," she told them. "These invites won't hand out themselves!"

I stared after her retreating back, shaking my head. Ashley was one of a kind. Thank goodness.

All thoughts of Ashley left my head as soon as I saw my friends gathered together outside. Jessica was hugging everyone like she was never going to see them again. When I broke into the circle she threw her arms around my neck. "I'll miss you guys so much!" she said.

I patted her on the back. "We'll iChat," I promised. "Plus, you'll be having so much fun learning to surf you won't even think about us."

Jessica brightened. "That's right!" she said.

We all rolled our eyes. That was so Jessica! After promising to bring us each back some chocolate-covered macadamia nuts, Jess headed home to finish packing. Amy and Heather left together next, goofily waving and blowing kisses. Finally, it was just me and Becky.

"Hey, guess what I just found out," I said, remembering Ashley's party. But Becky wasn't paying attention to me. She was staring into the distance, a funny look on her face. I wasn't used to my very focused BFF spacing out, so it took me a moment to realize what was going on.

Incoming boy, ten o'clock.

"Hey, Becky," said Matt, grinning goofily.

"Hey, Matt," said Becky shyly.

"So I was wondering if maybe . . ." Matt's voice trailed off and he glanced in my direction, clearly embarrassed that I was there.

I stepped back to give them some privacy — and banged right into someone.

I grimaced, hoping against hope it wasn't . . .

"Hello, Delfartcushion," Bob said. And then he laughed so hard at his own joke he nearly choked. He must have been working on that one for weeks. I watched him, completely unamused.

"At least you crack *yourself* up," I said, shaking my head.

Bob Zimmer was Matt's best friend and the Most Annoying Boy in the Entire Seventh Grade. Correction. The Most Annoying Boy in Sarah Josepha Hale Middle School. If there was ever a vote, I'm sure it would be unanimous.

But, I realized, Bob hadn't quite been himself since Matt started crushing on my best friend. I decided to take pity on him and gave him a sympathetic glance.

He looked at me in alarm. "What, do you have a crush on me, or something?" he said rather loudly.

"As if!" I sputtered. "Go away, Bob," I said. With any luck I wouldn't have to see him again until September.

Becky, who had been in deep conversation with Matt, missed the whole thing. She said her good-byes and headed over to me, her face glowing. "Hey, my mom's here to pick me up. You want a ride home?"

"That's all right," I said. "I don't mind walking."

"We'll get together before I leave," she said. "I promise. And I'm really sorry about not celebrating your birthday today. I'll make it up to you, I swear."

"It's okay," I assured her. "I'll talk to you later."

After Becky had zoomed off in her mom's bright red car, I scanned the front of the school for stragglers. Not that I was looking for anyone, mind you. But there was one person I wouldn't mind saying good-bye to before I left. . . .

My face lit up as I spotted him, leaning against the handrail by the front steps. He waved to me and I headed toward him.

"Hey," I said when I got close enough to Hamilton Baldwin, the newest and cutest boy in the school. I had received text confirmation (from Hamilton himself) that he liked me, but we had never managed to hang out together since then. Now seemed like a pretty good time for him to ask me to do something this summer. And I was totally prepared to say yes.

"Hey, Del," he said. "Can you believe it's the last day of school?"

"I can't," I said. "It went so fast." I took a deep breath. *Here goes nothing*, I thought. "So, any plans this summer?" I asked, I hoped, quite casually.

I stole a quick glance at him. Tall, longish sandy-blond hair, and deep blue eyes. Supercute, funny, and nice. There was just one problem, one that was pretty hard to ignore: Hamilton just happens to be the son of the owner of the only other flower shop in Elwood Falls — Fleur: brand-new, sleek, large, and in the mall. The complete opposite of our store, which is small, cozy, and in the middle of town. I don't make things easy for myself, do I?

Hamilton frowned. "Oh, I'll be pretty busy. I'm going to visit my dad for a couple of weeks in August. And we'll have a few visitors, including my grandparents. How about you?"

"Maine for two weeks," I said. "Then . . . the usual stuff." I didn't want to mention the time I'd spend working at Petal Pushers. After some near disasters, Hamilton and I had made a promise not to discuss business, ever. It was the only way we could stay friends.

"But I'll be in town for the next couple of weeks," I hinted.

"Great!" said Hamilton. "Well, I guess I'll see you around!"

My heart sank. "See you around, Hamilton," I replied.

As he turned to leave, I could see something sticking out of his back pocket. Was it his report card? I looked closer and saw the familiar gold lettering.

It was an invitation to Ashley's party.

Great. Just great.

Chapter Two

"I'm home!" I called as I pushed open the front door. I could tell by the haphazard pile of shoes in the hallway that my sisters and my parents were all there, too. I nudged one of Poppy's bright orange Crocs out of the way and stepped inside.

The kitchen door swung open and Mom stuck out her head. Her light brown hair peeked out from under a green scarf. "Hey, Del!" she called.

"You're home early," I said, hoping everything was okay at the store.

"Wouldn't miss a moment of our" — she paused — "eighth annual last-day-of-school barbecue. Come help us get ready!"

"I'll just be a minute!" I said. I laughed to myself as I headed up the stairs. Mom was right. We'd been having this barbecue every year since my last day of kindergarten.

In my tidy bedroom — the only neat room in the entire house, I might add — I emptied my backpack, placing my folders and notebooks on my spotless desk. In the bathroom, I removed Poppy's squirting rubber octopus from the sink, washed my hands and face, and pulled my hair into a ponytail. Then I changed into a pair of terry-cloth polka-dotted shorts and my favorite, old Hello Kitty T-shirt. Feeling refreshed, I headed down to the kitchen.

"Welcome home, Del!" my sister Rose sang out. She may just be ten years old, but Rose is already a budding actress and does everything dramatically, from brushing her teeth to opening the refrigerator. She was slicing lemons in half on a cutting board, her blonde hair twisted in a bun on top of her head. Her twin, Aster, pale and dark-haired, looked even more serious than usual as she worked the juicer, concentrating on getting every drop out of the lemons.

"Lemonade!" I said appreciatively. A glass of pale yellow lemonade with flecks of lemon pulp, tart and sweet and jingling with ice cubes, means summer to me, no doubt about it. "Hurry it up!" I told them. "I have a pow-erful thirst!"

"Easy, sailor," said Aster sassily. I laughed.

Poppy, my five-year-old sister, held a cucumber in one hand and a big bumpy heirloom tomato in the other. "Can we make a salad together?" she asked me, hopping up and down excitedly. "It will be pondiferous!"

"Pondiferous?" I asked.

"It means amazing," said Rose with a shrug. "Poppy's into making up new words now."

"Oh," I said. Poppy is always up to something interest-ing. "Sure!" I told her, though I usually hate being on salad duty. Too much washing and chopping for me. But it was apparently a big thrill for Poppy, so I feigned enthusiasm for her sake. She dragged over the step stool so she'd be at counter level. I hauled out the salad spinner and we began tearing off lettuce leaves for soaking and rinsing.

The screen door opened with a squeal, and Dad came in, an apron tied around his waist. GRILLMASTER, the apron proclaimed across his chest in large, red letters. I hid my smile. Well, we'd see about that. Dad was, to be kind, not the best chef in town. And wouldn't you know it, he really loved to cook.

"Del!" he said, giving me a kiss on my cheek. "How was the last day of school?"

"Fine," I said, choosing to keep both my forgotten birthday and my non-invitation to Ashley's party to myself.

"Good," he replied. "Hey, have you seen the tongs? I tore the place up looking for them, but nobody seems to know where they are."

With a sigh I walked over to the drawer where we kept the barbecue utensils, pulled it open, and fished out the tongs. "Here you go," I said.

Dad grinned. "What would we do without you, Detail Del?" He headed back outside, snapping the tongs together.

"Try the lemonade, DD," said Rose, offering me a glass.

I took a sip. "Needs a little more sugar," I said. "Otherwise perfect."

Mom emerged from the pantry, holding a blue glass pitcher that had belonged to her grandmother Violet and a bunch of deep purple hydrangeas she had brought home from the store. She filled the pitcher with cold water, a tablespoon of sugar (flower food), and a tablespoon of bleach (to avoid bacterial growth). Then she expertly cut the stems at an angle, removed any of the leaves that might be underwater, and began arranging the flowers.

I felt a rush of joy just watching her; I have always loved the sight and smell of flowers, not to mention the happiness that comes from arranging them just so. I guess it makes sense that I come from a family of florists.

Mom had been running Petal Pushers since my grandparents had left for Florida two months before. Mom loved working again and was super creative with the flower arrangements. But the store was a lot of work. I'd been helping out after school and on weekends, and I'd be able to help out more now that school was out. Dad, a college professor, was off for the summer, too. He'd be pitching in as well, but his main job was going to be Mr. Mom, since summer camp for three girls was just too expensive.

"Nice flowers, Mom," I said. I especially love hydrangeas — so abundant-looking and cheerful. There's something old-fashioned about them, too. And if you change the water in the vase every day they can last for weeks. You know that saying about how the shoe-maker's kids always go barefoot? Well, it's not true about florist's families, at least not ours. We nearly always have a bouquet of something colorful and fragrant in our house.

Mom sniffed the air. "Oh no," she said. "Has Dad overcooked the meat again?"

We rushed out the door to find Dad whistling cheer-fully as he sliced the meat. "I hope you like it well done," he said.

"I think he means incinerated," Aster said softly from behind me.

So we all sat down to a meal of grayish meat, potato salad, and Poppy's and my salad. The meat certainly was chewy, but I discovered that extra steak sauce made it borderline edible.

"So?" Mom looked at us girls expectantly. "Last day of school? Grades?"

Everyone had done well. Aster's grades were a bit better than Rose's. And mine were the best of all. Not that I'm bragging or anything.

Mom stood up and walked around the table giving us hugs and kisses. "I am so proud of my girls," she said with a sniff. "We have a lot to celebrate."

"Hear! Hear!" said Dad. "Three of my girls graduating on one day!" It was true; tomorrow, Poppy would be graduating from kindergarten, and Rose and Aster from elementary. Dad paused, and got that "I'm about to quote someone" look in his eye. " 'The roots of education are bitter, but the fruit is sweet.' " He took a sip of lemonade. "Aristotle."

"Are you all excited for tomorrow?" Mom asked.

Poppy's eyes were shining. "Yes!" she said. "My very first cap and gown ever!"

"I can't wait to walk across that stage and get my diploma," said Rose. "It's going to be awesome, just you wait." She grinned at her twin. "Right, Aster?"

Aster gave a small nod of agreement.

That reminded me. "How have graduation orders been?" I asked Mom.

I was still worried about something my great-aunt Lily, who co-owns Petal Pushers, had said a couple weeks ago: *Just remember, you're going to need all the help*

24

you can get to keep the store afloat through the summer!
Aunt Lily is a glass-half-empty kind of lady, but she
knows what she's talking about. I wanted to make sure
we were doing okay, especially since we were closing the
store for two whole weeks to go on our Maine vacation.

"Pretty good," Mom said. "The graduation orders are
all finished and ready for pickup tomorrow morning. I
told everyone we'd be open from eight till nine thirty.
Then we'll close for the day and hit the graduations!"

Our town has almost all of its graduations on the same
day, for some reason. Kindergarten, fifth grade, eighth
grade, and high school. Poppy would graduate in the
morning, Rose and Aster in the afternoon. The eighth
graders were right after that, and the high schoolers came
last. Luckily, I had reminded Mom to make a dinner reservation at Oscar's well in advance. It was the fanciest
restaurant in town and very popular. The fact that
Mom did their weekly flowers probably helped us score a
table, too.

"And then two more weeks and we'll be in Maine," I
said excitedly. I could practically smell the ocean air and
taste the lobster rolls.

"When do we leave?" Rose asked.

"July sixth," I reminded her. "Right after the store closes."

I noticed Mom's furrowed brow.

"That *was* the plan," I said, looking from Mom to Dad in confusion. "Right?"

Mom bit her lip. "I have something to tell you all. I got a call today about doing the flowers for an anniversary party," she said, gazing down at the tablecloth.

"That's great news!" said Dad.

"A big party?" I asked hopefully.

"Pretty big," Mom said brightly. Then she took a deep breath. "There's only one problem . . . it's on July seventh."

I froze, my lemonade glass halfway to my waiting mouth. It couldn't be. "But . . . that's my birthday!" I cried. This would ruin everything. Instead of being on the road to Maine on Friday, we'd be up late that night assembling the centerpieces. Then the next day we'd have to deliver them, set them up, and take care of any last-minute issues. Not exactly the birthday I had planned. I mean, one of the good parts about being a kid is that you don't have to work on your birthday, right?

Mom ran her hand through her hair. "I know, I know," she said. "But I couldn't say no. We need the business. Especially since we're closing for two weeks." She leaned forward and looked into my eyes. "Delly, I'm sorry. I'll make it up to you."

"That's the second time I've heard that today," I said in a sharp voice that almost didn't sound like mine. I could feel my face getting warm. Usually, I am all for putting business first. But it was my birthday. My *thirteenth* birthday. "This is completely unfair!"

Everyone was staring at me like I was a two-headed calf at a state fair. I don't lose my cool very often, so when I do, people seem to pay attention.

"What's wrong with Del?" I heard Poppy whisper to Rose.

"She's totally losing it!" said Rose, looking slightly fascinated.

"I am *not* losing it!" I said defensively, though I kind of felt like I was about to.

"Well, what time is the party?" Dad asked Mom.

"It's in the afternoon," Mom said, her eyes trained on my face. "So we could be on the road by four o'clock," she said. "Five at the latest."

Dad turned to me. "See? We can be in Maine in time for twin lobsters at Brown's for your birthday dinner!"

I sighed. They just didn't get it.

Everyone began chattering away about graduation as we cleared the table. "Let's play a game before bed!" Rose begged, but I said I was tired and I headed upstairs as soon as the last fork was in the dishwasher.

I lay down on my bed and tried to read for a while. But I couldn't concentrate. There was a lump in my throat and my heart was heavy. All I could think was: *I'm turning thirteen. And nobody seems to care. Not my friends, not my family . . . not anybody.*

Chapter Three

"Wake up, Del, wake up! It's graduation day!" Poppy's squeaky voice was even more high-pitched than usual.

I groaned and pulled the sheets over my head. "Poppy, it's only . . ." I opened one eye to peer at my bedside clock. "Six thirty!" I sighed. My first school-free day and I was up at the crack of dawn. Plus, I was still feeling cranky about the bombshell Mom had dropped last night.

"Today's the day I get my dip . . . dip . . ."

"Diploma," I finished for her.

"Yes, that thing," she said with a nod. "I'm so excited I can't sleep anymore. Let's go get some breakfast!"

I tried a new angle. "Wouldn't you rather have breakfast with your fellow graduates, Aster and Rose?" I suggested.

Poppy considered this for a moment. Then she shook her head. "Nope."

Oh well. I yawned, stood up, and headed downstairs with my little sister.

"Oh jeez, Poppy," I said as she began calling out numbers. "Do you really have to count every step this morning?"

Poppy gave me a dirty look and raced back to the top of the stairs. I had made her lose her count. I slipped ahead of her and headed downstairs.

"Twenty-two!" she announced when she made it to the kitchen. By that time, I had already poured her a bowl of Cheerios and a glass of orange juice. As I grabbed a banana to slice it, she said, "Open it like a monkey!"

"Oh, that's right," I said, flipping it upside down and pinching the bottom open. Poppy had seen that YouTube video: "How To Peel a Banana Like a Monkey" and now insisted that we all follow suit. I was poised to slice the banana into her cereal when she said, "I don't eat bananas in my cereal anymore."

"Now you tell me!" I said. Five-year-olds! I shrugged and took a bite of the banana. Poppy was right. The top *did* make a nice handle.

Poppy settled herself at our old wooden kitchen table.

She picked up her spoon, looked up at me, and smiled. "Today is the most important day of my life, Del," she said completely seriously. "I'm a little dipsiddish."

I looked at her quizzically.

"That means nervous," she explained. I stifled a grin and sat down across from her. I took a sip of juice. "It *is* an important day, Poppy," I agreed. "But there's no need to be nervous." She gave me a look. "I mean dipsiddish. It's a piece of cake."

Poppy's face lit up. "I get cake?"

"That's an expression," I told her. "It means it's easy, nothing to worry about."

"Oh," said Poppy, disappointed.

One by one, my family began to make their way downstairs. Dad shuffled in and went right to the coffee-maker without a word. He was useless without his morning caffeine. After a couple of minutes, the rich, breakfast-y aroma of brewing coffee filled the air. Dad magically perked up at the smell.

Rose and Aster came down together, both looking sleepy. Rose was in her pink-and-white pj's, and Aster was in one of her many black nightgowns.

Mom came down last, just as the coffeemaker began beeping. "Coffee!" she said, her eyes lighting up. Dad poured her a cup first. He added just the right amount of milk and handed it to her.

"Now this is heaven," he said, pouring his own cup. I swear, I will never understand grown-ups and their need for coffee.

Mom took a sip. "I know," she replied. She sat down and wrapped both hands around the mug. She stared at me from across the table. "Del, I am so sorry your birthday got all messed up."

I nodded. I wanted to tell my mom not to worry, but I couldn't keep the frown off my face.

"So I was thinking that maybe you guys could leave Friday as planned. I could do the party myself and take the bus up Saturday night to meet you," she suggested.

I was about to consider that when Poppy freaked out. "No, Mommy! We can't go without you!" she shrieked.

Mom turned to me. "Del?" she said.

I was torn. Obviously, I wanted Mom with us. But I really didn't like the idea of having to work on my birthday. Still, I am the reasonable one in the family. And part of that is being, well, reasonable. Even when you don't feel like it.

"It's okay, Mom," I said. "I don't want you to be by yourself. We'll still be in Maine in time for an awesome birthday dinner." I hoped I sounded like I meant it.

"Thanks, Del," said Mom gratefully. Dad nodded at me and went back to his paper.

Everybody was ignoring our Boston terrier, Buster, who was whining and hitting his food bowl with his paw, so I fed him. He wolfed down his breakfast and then started jumping up and down for his morning walk. I ran upstairs, threw on some sweatpants, a T-shirt, and flip-flops, and headed outside, snapping on his leash.

The house was strangely quiet as I walked back in the kitchen door with the now calm Buster. *That's funny,* I thought, *for a disorganized household, graduation day is going pretty smoothly.* But then I realized how wrong I was. The kitchen table was littered with dirty coffee cups, juice glasses, bowls, and plates. A bowl of cereal had been knocked over, and milk and soggy Os were dripping onto the floor. Buster ran over and began lapping it up. I chased him away, picked up a sponge, and started cleaning.

When the dishwasher was loaded and the table was clean, I headed back upstairs to get ready. I found Mom tearing apart the linen closet, Rose, Poppy, and Dad standing there watching her.

"Mom forgot we have to iron our gowns!" wailed Rose.

"Del, have you seen the iron?" Mom asked me, her arms full of towels.

"What's an iron?" said Poppy.

"Exactly," I said. I turned to Mom. "I keep the iron in my room," I explained. *Because I'm the only one who ever uses it,* I added silently.

I set up the ironing board in the upstairs hallway and plugged in the iron. "Dad, you're going to have to do it," I told him. "Mom and I have to get to the store. We're supposed to open in half an hour!"

Mom slapped her hand to her head. "You're right! I'll just hop in the shower."

"Great," said Dad, looking at the ironing board like it was some sort of torture device.

"Has anyone seen my black dress?" asked Aster, poking her head out of the room she shares with Rose.

"You'll have to be more specific," Mom responded.

"I can't find my ruffly socks!" shouted Poppy at the same time that Rose called, "Has anyone seen my purple bicycle shorts?"

Mom turned to Dad. "It's all yours, dear," she said, shutting the bathroom door behind her.

Dad looked at me, his eyes pleading. "Take me with you," he said only slightly jokingly.

"Sorry, Dad," I said with a grin. "You heard Mom. It's all yours."

He shook his head and picked up the iron. "Three graduations in one day. That's two too many!" He licked his finger and tapped it on the iron to see if it was hot enough. It made a satisfying sizzle. He started ironing graduation gown number one. I just hoped he wouldn't scorch it.

There were two moms, a dad, and a grandma waiting, rather impatiently, outside the store when we arrived. They picked up two corsages, a bouquet, and one funny flower face. Mom had come up with the flower face — a large chrysanthemum with a pipe-cleaner smiley face and a big fat bumblebee on it — just for the kindergarten graduation. It was supercute. That's my mom for you — always thinking up something new and fun with flowers.

The morning was busy with pickups and some drop-in customers. Luckily, we had made an extra supply of ready-made bouquets the night before. Finally, at a quarter to ten, we had to close our doors. We would just make Poppy's graduation if we rushed. Mom was about to lock the door when I remembered something.

"Our flowers!" I shouted. Imagine if Poppy, Rose, and Aster were flowerless for their graduation. That would be terrible! I ran back inside to get the special flowers we had made — a smiley mum for Poppy, a bouquet of pink roses for the bright and cheerful Rose, and these almost-black roses with yellow stripes for the dark and pensive Aster. Mom locked the door behind me and we hit the pavement running.

Luckily, kindergarten graduations always seem to start late. There was time to slip into the seats that Dad had saved for us on the aisle in the middle of the auditorium.

Mom and I grinned at each other as we caught our breath. We had made it!

We stood as "Pomp and Circumstance" began to play. I almost started giggling as the kindergartners began straggling down the aisle — such a serious song for such a tiny bunch of kids. They looked so big-eyed and solemn. Poppy didn't crack a smile until she looked up and realized she was standing right next to me. Then she punched me in the leg. "Hey, Del!" she said excitedly.

Principal Shaw, who had been *my* principal way back in elementary school, gave a quick speech about children being our future, yada yada yada. Then the kids walked across the auditorium floor, accepted their diplomas, shook the principal's hand, and then he asked them each a question: "What do you want to be when you grow up?"

That's right! I remembered. The principal always asked each kid that question at graduation day. It was a tradition. I wondered how many kids would actually end up being what they said they wanted to be. I doubted, for example, that Carmine Belloni still wanted to be a cowboy. I realized I had no idea what Poppy might actually say.

America Anderson wanted to be a ballerina. Jordan Billings, an ice-cream man. Next, it was Poppy's turn. She solemnly walked across the floor, accepted her diploma, and shook the principal's hand.

"And what do you want to be when you grow up, Poppy?" he asked.

Complete silence. Poppy looked panicked for a moment.

"Poppy?" the principal prodded. She scrunched up her face, thinking hard.

Poppy, say something, I thought. *A veterinarian. An astronaut. A teacher!*

"Um . . ." Poppy began.

The principal was starting to look a little impatient. "Yes?" he said.

"When I grow up, I want to be . . ." She looked around wildly.

I tried sending her brain waves. *A doctor. A librarian. A sanitation worker!*

"A . . . a . . . a . . . a zebra!" Poppy finally said.

"How creative!" said the principal, giving Poppy a

gentle pat on her back to guide her toward her class. The auditorium burst into laughter. Poppy's shoulders sagged as she slumped in her seat.

Mom and I gave each other quizzical looks. Zebra? Where had that come from?

The rest of the ceremony went off without a hitch. The other kids all gave human answers and soon all the five-year-olds had a diploma in hand. As they lined up to sing their farewell song, "You Are My Sunshine," I stole a glance at Poppy's face. She looked decidedly unhappy.

After the kids marched back down the aisle, I pushed my way out of the auditorium. I emerged to find a spread of coffee, juice, and a large sheet cake. I grabbed a slice and searched the crowd to find Poppy. This would surely cheer her up.

"Hey, I said it would be a piece of cake — and here it is," I said, handing her the plate.

"No thanks," said Poppy.

I've never known my little sister to turn down anything with sugar, not to mention frosting roses.

"What's wrong, Pops?" I asked.

"Everyone laughed at me," she said, her lower lip thrust out.

"They weren't laughing at you, they were laughing with you," I said lamely. Even as I said the words, I knew they wouldn't work.

"Except *I* wasn't laughing," Poppy pointed out.

Soon the rest of the family found us. Mom handed Poppy her mum, which was different from all the other smiley faces because Mom had glued a pair of false eyelashes on in place of the plain old black pipe-cleaner eyes. Poppy was delighted with her fancy flower and gave it a big hug.

I smiled at Mom. Looked like the crisis had passed.

We lingered over cake and juice until the kindergartners and their families left and the fifth-grade graduates began to arrive. "Round two!" said Dad. We wished Rose and Aster good luck and headed back into the auditorium.

I looked around the room, seeing familiar faces from town, as well as some kids from my grade whose siblings were graduating, too. I thought about next year, when I was going to be an eighth grader. And after that, high school. Our middle school combined with the schools from several other towns, so there would be lots of new kids to meet. Exciting. And a little scary.

Poppy leaned over. "I'm feeling a little blazonky that Gran and Gramps missed my graduation," she said.

I frowned. "Um . . . does that mean sad?"

"Yes," she said impatiently. She may as well have added "duh!"

I nodded. We used to get together with Gran and Gramps once a week for dinner, movie, and ice-cream-sundae night. Plus, I worked in their store every Saturday. This was the first big occasion that they had missed. It felt weird not to have Gran sniffling away next to Mom (they are both total criers) and Gramps handing out hard candies just when we started to feel fidgety.

We stood for the procession, sat through a song that was translated into sign language, and listened to some speeches. I stared off into space, wishing for one of Gramps's root-beer barrels while the assistant principal droned on way longer than seemed fair. I'm a little embarrassed to say that I texted back and forth with Becky about how bored I was until Mom gave me the elbow and made me shut my phone off.

Finally, it was time to hand out diplomas. "This year we've decided to try something new," said Principal Shaw. "Each student will be given the chance to send a personal message to their family and friends after they receive their diploma." I sat up with interest. Was this what Rose meant when she said that graduation was going to be "awesome"?

Kenny Aboud thanked his parents and his "peeps." Grace Adderly shouted "I did it, Mom!" and Chris Balsam spoke of his gratitude to Mrs. Miller for not making him repeat fifth grade. Asha Bhanghoo thanked her dog, her mom, and her grandfather, in that order, and waved and blew kisses like a beauty queen.

"Aster Bloom!" called the principal. I leaned forward. What would my silent sister have to say?

Aster walked across the stage, looking uncomfortable in her pale blue cap and gown. She was probably wishing they were black. She accepted her diploma, shook Mr. Shaw's hand, and cleared her throat.

"A graduation poem," she said.

"Wearing caps and gowns,
Now our lives are no longer
Elementary."

The principal looked like he wasn't quite sure what to say. There was complete silence in the auditorium. Then Dad let out a loud whoop. "Great haiku, Aster!" he shouted. So mortifying!

Next it was Rose's turn. After accepting her diploma, she simply said, "Thank you, everyone."

Is that it? I wondered. How boring. How unlike Rose.

Then she put her diploma in her mouth, dropped her hands to the ground, and turned three perfect cartwheels in a row across the stage. I caught a flash of the purple bicycle shorts, which I guess she had located. The crowd cheered.

I shook my head. Never a dull moment with my family, that was for sure.

At the end of the ceremony, the graduates simultaneously threw their hats into the air with a huge cheer. One hit the assistant principal, who had given the boring speech, right in the forehead. I wondered if it had been on purpose.

Poppy clutched her smiley mum the whole way home, touching mailboxes and flowers and our neighbor's beagle with it like it was a magic wand. Mom and Dad held hands and talked about parent stuff and Rose and Aster walked side by side. I lagged behind, thinking about the summer. I wondered what Hamilton was doing right then. Maybe eating lunch or skateboarding in the park.

We had a couple hours to kill before dinner, so Dad took a nap and the rest of us watched *Ponyo*. Then, when Dad woke up, we piled in the car to head to Oscar's. Great-aunt Lily was going to meet us there. Mom had invited her to the ceremonies as well, but she had opted for dinner only. Smart lady.

When we pushed open the heavy oak doors to Oscar's, I was surprised to discover that the usual hushed atmosphere was buzzing with activity. The entryway was filled with students from kindergarten to high school, all there to celebrate with their families. I peeked into the dining room and took in the flickering candles, the gleaming silverware and crystal, the starched white tablecloths, and the tuxedoed waiters bustling about. I felt the familiar awkwardness that always comes over me when I'm in fancy places, like I'm going to trip in front of everyone. And even though I knew it couldn't possibly be true, I felt like all eyes were on me as I crossed the floor to our table.

Just my luck. I hadn't been paying attention as we sat down and ended up with an empty seat to my right. Poppy was on the other side of the empty chair. "Hey, Poppy," I said casually. "Want to sit next to me?" But Aster, on Poppy's other side, knew exactly what I was up to.

"She's staying right where she is," Aster said with a tight smile. I looked at my parents to see if they would be willing to trade, but they were both suddenly very interested in their menus. Nobody wanted to be stuck sitting next to Aunt Lily.

We had already ordered our drinks when the maître d' led her to our table, my great-aunt nodding to the other diners like she was the Queen of England. It's true, she does know tons of people through all her charity work. Not to mention her advanced age. Did I say that?

When Aunt Lily's drink arrived, Dad proposed a

toast. "To our graduates," he said with a grin. "Rose, Poppy, and Aster. You girls have made us all so proud of you this year!"

"To our graduates," we echoed.

Aunt Lily folded her hands together. "I heard there were some real high jinks at graduation today," she said, looking pointedly at Rose.

Rose gulped. Old Lady Mafia strikes again! I wondered which sweet-looking grandma in the audience had immediately phoned Aunt Lily to report *that* tidbit.

"The girls were very entertaining" was all Mom said.

Aunt Lily raised her eyebrows. "In my day, children behaved with decorum, especially at an important event like a graduation," she said. She next set her sights on Poppy. "And how was your graduation, young lady?" she asked.

"Good!" said Poppy. "Mommy made me a smiley face!" She reached under her chair and grabbed her flower, which was looking a little worse for wear. Brandishing the long stem like a sword, she bopped Aunt Lily on the head, nearly knocking off her hat. Aunt Lily dresses like someone from a time gone by. No Adidas tracksuits for her like some of the senior citizens in town — she's always wearing hats and gloves and fancy, tweedy-looking suits, no matter what the weather.

"Lovely," said Aunt Lily through clenched teeth. She gazed at Poppy. "So, is it true that you want to be a *giraffe* when you grow up?"

"It was a zebra," Poppy corrected her shamefacedly.

Oh no. I looked at Mom, my eyes wide. Would Poppy get upset all over again?

Yes, she would. Her lip began to tremble. "I couldn't think of anything else," she whispered.

Mom gave Aunt Lily a nervous glance. "It does seem a little early to decide what you want to be," she said. "I used to want to be a zookeeper," she added with a laugh. "And that didn't exactly work out!"

"That's right," added Dad. "Nobody needs to know their career when they graduate from kindergarten! It's absurd!"

Aunt Lily started at him icily. "It's an Elwood Falls tradition," she explained. Dad was the only one at the table "from away" (as we say in New England) and who hadn't graduated from Elwood Falls Elementary. "I knew I wanted to be a flower shop owner and run various charities when I grew up," she said. "I don't think it's absurd at all."

Poppy poked me in the arm. "What did you say when you graduated?"

"I'm pretty sure I wanted to be a florist," I admitted sheepishly.

"And Rose?"

"I wanted to be an actress," she said. "Of course."

"Poet," offered Aster.

"See, you all knew," said Poppy sadly. "Everyone knew except for me."

I opened my mouth to say something reassuring to my little sister, but the waiter had appeared to recite the evening's specials. *Don't waste your time on me,* I thought. I knew what I'd be having: a small mixed green salad and Chicken Oscar, my favorite. It comes with ham and cheese stuffed inside. I know I should try new things, but it's just so good. Rose, I knew, would order the weirdest thing on the menu.

Sure enough. "I'll have the escargot for my appetizer. And I think I'll try the steak tartare!" She smiled and handed the waiter her menu.

I looked at her, horrified. Did she know she just ordered snails in butter sauce and raw beef? Mom leaned over and whispered in Rose's ear. Rose made a face and grabbed her menu back. She consulted with Mom and decided on French onion soup and filet mignon.

Once everyone had ordered, silence fell over the table. My overly talkative family was very quiet in Aunt Lily's presence. I sighed. If only Gran and Gramps were here.

"So, will you be attending the Fourth of July festivities, Aunt Lily?" Dad asked politely.

"I haven't missed them in seventy years," said Aunt Lily. "I won't be starting this year."

"Rose is going to sing at the pre-fireworks show," said Mom.

"'America the Beautiful'!" Rose squealed.

Aunt Lily looked suitably impressed. "That's quite an honor, Rose," she said.

"We're going to have a picnic dinner on the field before the show," said Mom. "You're welcome to join us."

Don't say yes, don't say yes, I thought.

"Mom makes the best fried chicken!" Rose offered. I sent her a death-ray glare.

49

"Thank you," Aunt Lily said stiffly. "But I don't enjoy picnics."

I gave her a funny look. How weird. Fourth of July is my favorite time of year. I like it almost as much as Christmas-slash-Hanukkah, as we call it in my house, since we celebrate both. And I can't think of a better place to celebrate the Fourth of July than Elwood Falls, New Hampshire. It's just so . . . all-American. Kids weave red and white and blue ribbons in their bicycle spokes. The high school band marches with the big drums pounding so deep you can feel it in the pit of your stomach, and high-stepping majorettes throwing their batons so impossibly high in the air that you hold your breath until they catch them. Plus, Fourth of July is so close to my birthday that I feel like the fireworks are just for me. I couldn't wait.

The waiter returned with our appetizers and set my salad down in front of me. It looked delicious. There was just one problem. I had no idea which fork I was supposed to use. There were several lined up on the left side of my plate. Did you start with the outside fork or take the closest one and work your way out? I actually broke out into a cold sweat. I usually don't care about this stuff at all, but sitting next to Great-aunt Lily, chief of the manners police and a pretty scary old lady to boot, will do that to you. I stared hungrily at my salad. Then someone kicked me. Not hard, but hard enough. I looked up to see Mom grinning at me from across the table. She looked pointedly at my forks. I put a finger on the inside fork. She shook her head. I moved to the outside, smaller fork. She smiled. I gave her a grateful grin back.

The rest of dinner went on without incident. Mom told Aunt Lily all about our vacation, and I was relieved when Mom didn't invite her along. The food was crazy delicious and I polished off my whole entrée. Even though we were stuffed, we all ordered dessert. I had something called floating islands, which sounds more interesting than it actually is, trust me. But it tasted pretty good, anyway.

"We totally forgot to tell Aunt Lily our good news!" said Dad as he poured cream into his coffee.

"Yes?" said Aunt Lily.

"We have a party in July!" he told her.

"Oh," said Aunt Lily, leaning forward. "Whose party? The Edwards girl?"

Wow. Aunt Lily does *know everybody's business,* I thought. Even Ashley's bash was on her radar!

"No, Mr. and Mrs. McGillicuddy's golden anniversary," Mom provided.

Aunt Lily sat up stiffly. "Oh, the McGillicuddys," she said dismissively. "So, did you hear that the town hall is getting a new roof? Well, I'll tell you, it's about time. . . ."

Why does Aunt Lily not like the McGillicuddys? I wondered. I debated bringing the party up again, just to see what she would say. But then I chickened out.

After dinner, Poppy was so tired Dad slung her over his shoulder as we made our way to the car. Luckily, we had a minivan so we could fit everyone. We dropped Aunt Lily off, waited until Dad had walked her to her door, and headed for home.

"I have a surprise," said Mom when we walked inside. It turned out to be an iChat with Gran and Gramps! Poppy, who had been dozing on Dad's shoulder, perked right up. We rushed to Dad's office and huddled around the computer.

When they appeared on the screen we all burst into

laughter. Gran and Gramps were sitting there, graduation caps on their heads!

"Happy graduation, girls!" they chorused.

"Where did you get those?" asked Mom, wiping tears from her eyes from laughing so hard.

"We borrowed them from our neighbors," said Gran. "Glad you enjoyed our surprise!"

The connection was pretty good, with only a tiny time delay and minimal freezing. We filled them in on the day's events, including our fancy dinner. We left out the zebra thing, though we did tell them all about Aster's poem and Rose's cartwheels. Gran and Gramps got a good laugh out of that one.

Then I thought of something. "Hey," I said. "Why doesn't Aunt Lily like the McGillicuddys?" I asked.

"Geraldine and Jerome?" Gramps said. "They're so nice. Why wouldn't Lily like them?"

But Gran knew exactly what I was talking about. "It's so sad," she said. "Lily and Geraldine were the very best of friends in high school, and they were always close after. Then something happened. I'm not sure what it was, but it couldn't have been good. They haven't spoken in fifteen years."

"Hmmm," I said. "Well, the McGillicuddys are having an anniversary party and we're doing the flowers."

"Oh, how lovely!" said Gran. "I'll have to send them a card!"

But then her face turned serious. "Girls," she said, "I'm sorry we missed your graduations. But we just couldn't get away. The Isaacs are coming back in two weeks and we still haven't found a new place to live."

I could feel a lump forming in my throat. I knew Gran and Gramps had decided to retire to Florida, but some part of me kept thinking they would return home. That they'd miss the store — and us — so much that they'd have to come back.

But, apparently, Key West was treating them just fine. They had worked hard in the store their whole lives and now they were kicking back and having fun. I couldn't begrudge them that. But it didn't make things any easier.

That night as I lay in bed, I had a terrible thought. Maybe Gran and Gramps were having so much fun in Florida they didn't miss us as much as we missed them.

Would Gran and Gramps ever come back — even just for a visit? I certainly hoped so.

I picked up my phone from my bedside table to check it before I turned out the light. No new messages. Sheesh. What was Hamilton waiting for? Then a smile stole across my face. Who said I had to wait for him to call me? I had his number. I could send him a text. Easy, right?

Forty-five minutes later, I had composed a text that combined the right amounts of interested, cool, and casual:

HEY, IT'S DEL. WANNA HANG OUT THIS WEEK?

It didn't take him as long to compose his reply:

SORRY, GOT PLANS. MAYBE ANOTHER TIME.

I stared at the text in disbelief. Was Hamilton Baldwin *blowing me off*?

I frowned and shut off the light. Between my messed-up birthday plans, my thoughts about Gran and Gramps, and Hamilton's dismissive text, there was only one word to describe how I felt.

Blazonky with a capital *B*.

Chapter Four

On Saturday, Mom and I left early to go to the store, leaving Dad at home with Aster, Rose, and Poppy. He had big plans — he was going to take them on a hike in the woods that morning. From the unhappy looks on my sisters' faces, I was pretty glad I wasn't attending Camp Dad that summer.

At Petal Pushers, I swept and Mom checked for messages. As the morning sunlight shone through the store windows, I could see how dirty they were. I crumpled up some newspaper, grabbed some of the new "green" cleaner we now used, and went to work on the inside. Scrubbing helped improve my bad mood from the night before.

Mom went through the flower cooler, discarding any flowers that were past their prime. We had two arrangements to make that day — an "It's a Girl!" bouquet and a belated high school graduation arrangement from some-one's out-of-town relative.

Mom emerged from the cooler, her hands filled with wilted blooms. She tossed them in the trash can. She looked glum.

"I still feel really bad about the anniversary party on your birthday," she said.

"Mom, it is what it is." I sighed. "Plus, if Mrs. McGillicuddy doesn't go to us, you know where she'll end up."

Mom sighed. "Fleur," she said. (Hamilton's mom's shop, in case you haven't been paying attention.)

So far, Petal Pushers had not been feeling the competition from Fleur that much. We had scored the biggest wedding our town had ever seen, and had gotten most of the prom business. But customers can be fickle. We'd have to be on our toes to stay ahead. So I knew we couldn't afford to turn down any parties, no matter whose birthday they might fall on.

But that still didn't make me feel any better.

After we had restocked the ready-made bouquets, Mom started pulling out flowers from the cooler for the arrangements. Lots of pinks and whites for the "It's a Girl!" and some striking bright colors for the graduation arrangement. She selected two vases and put me to work on the graduation one. I felt the familiar surge of excitement as I began to assemble an arrangement in my head. I looked over at Mom, staring at her vase, her tongue sticking out in concentration. It was cozy working side by side at the worktable. I placed a red peony next to a double yellow freesia, changed my mind, and substituted a hot-pink zinnia.

Ring-a-ling-ling! The bell above the door rang. It was Dad, Poppy, Rose, and Aster, all looking sweaty and disgruntled.

"Back so soon?" I asked. "What's going on?"

Rose scowled. "The trail was all overgrown. We had to bail." She bent over to scratch her shin. "I think I got poison ivy," she complained. "Plus, Dad forgot to bring water."

"It was an adventure!" Dad said.

"I'll say," said Aster drily, reaching for a peony lying on the worktable. She sniffed it.

Poppy was being unusually quiet.

"Hey, Poppy," I said. "How was the hike?"

Poppy shrugged and leaned against the counter. Something was different about her. I squinted at my little sister. Normally, Poppy is not afraid of color and hasn't met a print she doesn't like. She often puts together some strange ensembles. But today she was in all black. *Odd choice for a hike,* I thought.

But before I could ask her what was up, the phone rang.

"Petal Pushers," said Mom brightly. "Oh hello, Eleanor, how are you?" Mom listened for a moment, then frowned. "You're calling about your *what*?" she said, sounding confused. She pressed the phone to her ear with her shoulder and used both hands to haul out the appointment book. She opened it and began flipping through the pages, looking puzzled.

"I'm dying!" said Rose dramatically as she fanned herself with a flower brochure.

"Shhhh!" I said, motioning to Mom. "I want to hear what's going on."

"Um, of course we're still on," Mom said, making a funny face at us. I stared at her. What in the world was going on? "Okay, so we'll see you this week. What day is good for you?" She scribbled something down in the appointment book. "Okay, good-bye," she said, then hung up the phone, her shoulders sagging.

"What happened?" I asked. "Is everything okay?"

Mom bit her lip. "I . . . I don't know what to say," she said.

That got everyone's attention. Five pairs of curious eyes were all focused on her.

"What?" I said. "Tell us!"

"That was Eleanor Edwards," she said. "Ashley's mom."

"Go on . . ." I said warily. This couldn't be good.

"And she called to ask about when she could come in to discuss the arrangements. . . ."

My heart sank. "For Ashley's birthday party?" I filled in.

Mom nodded, watching me carefully. "For Ashley's birthday party," she confirmed. "The same day as the anniversary party, and . . ."

She didn't need to say it. My birthday. I was speechless.

Mom scanned the book one more time. "I didn't know what else to do. I told her to come in this week." She sighed. "But there's nothing down in the appointment book. And she said she booked the date months in advance. But I don't see it! I never would have booked two events in one day!"

Dad cleared his throat as if he were about to say something. He looked very uncomfortable. Quickly, I grabbed the appointment book. Mom looked over my shoulder as I flipped through the pages. Nothing on July 7 of this year. But then I realized it was a two-year calendar. I turned the pages until I was at July 7 of the next year. And there, in Dad's loopy handwriting, one year in advance, it said, *Ashley Edwards's Birthday Party.*

"You've got to be kidding me!" I cried. "Dad!"

Dad grimaced. "I can't imagine how I did that," he said sheepishly.

Mom gave him a sympathetic look. "It could happen to anyone," she said.

I didn't say anything. But I thought, *Could it really?*

Mom turned to me, about to speak.

"I know what you're going to say," I said. "And Mom, you can't do two parties by yourself in one day. We have to stay." I closed my eyes and swallowed hard. I was basically giving up my birthday to help my worst enemy!

"Del, I . . ." Dad started to say.

"You what?" I said. "You completely ruined my birthday? You're right!"

His face fell. I felt completely awful. But I still felt overwhelmed with anger and disappointment. "I need to go for a walk," I said. "I'll be back."

"Del, wait," said Mom. "We'll . . . we'll . . . celebrate your birthday on Sunday instead. We'll have an amazing day!"

But I just walked right out. I was officially fed up. Ashley Edwards's birthday party was the straw that had broken the camel's back.

Chapter Five

"Oh, Del," said Becky, shaking her head. "That's terrible."

I nodded, then put my head on my knees and closed my eyes. I had headed to Becky's house as soon as I left the flower shop. We were sitting on her sunny front steps. But even Becky, the eternal optimist, couldn't put a positive spin on this one. However, the gasp she had let out when I told her what had happened had been very satisfying.

I lifted my head. "My mother suggested we pretend that *Sunday* is my birthday instead," I said bitterly.

Becky grimaced. "That's lame," she said.

"Totally," I agreed.

Becky stretched her bare feet across the top step. "Okay, imagine that you didn't have these two parties on your birthday. What would you do?"

"I'd also need to imagine that all my friends weren't leaving for the summer," I reminded her.

Becky grimaced again. "That, too," she said.

I smiled as I pictured the perfect summer birthday party. "It would be at the lake," I told her. "I'd set up picnic tables under a big tree and string the tree with white lights and paper lanterns."

Becky nodded and smiled. "Go on, it sounds great!" she said.

"I'd have a real New England clambake — we'd dig a hole and line it with rocks and light a fire. Then we'd fill it with seaweed and lobsters and steamers and corn on the cob and potatoes and onions and even eggs."

"Of course," agreed Becky. She knew the tradition of hard-boiled eggs at a clambake — the lobstermen used to carry the eggs in their pockets because they retained heat for so long and kept their hands warm on cold mornings. When the eggs cooled off, they would eat them with their lunch.

"I'd serve homemade lemonade in those big jars with the spigots, and the tables would have old quilts on them for tablecloths." I sat up straight. I was really on a roll. "The flowers would be wildflowers in Mason jars, filled with smooth stones at the bottom, and tied with twine at the top. We'd play games on the beach while the food cooked — horseshoes and scavenger hunts and three-legged races. And after dinner, we'd put on music and dance in the sand as the moon rose up."

"Wow, Del," said Becky. "What a great party." She smiled. "Maybe someday . . ."

"I know," I said. I sighed. "Maybe someday."

Becky touched my arm. "I know that your birthday plans are ruined, but you have to remember that your parents didn't do this on purpose," she said.

I pictured my dad's stricken face. "I know. I just wish they understood how I feel."

Becky giggled. "You ran out of the store. I think they get it now."

I grinned. "I guess you're right."

Becky looked at her watch. "I wish you could hang out with me all day," she said. "Especially since I'm leaving for camp tomorrow." She thought for a moment. "Hey, want to go shopping with me? I need to go to the sporting goods store and the drugstore for some last-minute things."

I gulped. I didn't know what would be more painful — shopping for tennis balls and dental floss or facing my family. "I think I should go back," I said, standing up. "I guess this is good-bye?" I made a sad face.

Becky climbed to her feet and shrugged resignedly. "I guess so," she said. She reached out and hugged me tight.

"Big Fat Friendship?" she said with a grin.

I returned the smile. When we were little, we had thought that's what BFF meant. "Big Fat Friendship," I replied, hugging her back. And then I headed off to make up with my family.

Everyone was still there when I got back to the store, so I apologized for yelling and running off. Dad apologized for messing up the dates. For the rest of the weekend, though, my family seemed to tiptoe around me, as though they feared I might explode again — but I didn't. Yes, I was still mad about everything, but I realized there was really nothing I could do. By Monday morning, when Mom and I were at the store again, things felt back to normal, or at least as normal as things can get among the Blooms.

"I hate to say this, Del," said Mom as she put the finishing touches on a "Happy Birthday" arrangement and I dusted the vase display. "But I'm kind of excited about doing the flowers for Ashley's birthday party."

The phrase "Ashley's birthday party" still sent a shudder down my spine, but I managed to shake it off. I put down the feather duster. "You're excited?" I asked incredulously. "You're joking, right?"

Mom shook her head. "No, I'm totally serious! I'm sure it's going to be a big event. I could go all out. I'd like to find some interesting containers at the flea market or, depending on the theme, maybe she'd want to do some sweet add-ins like fake butterflies or ladybugs, or seashells and seaweed . . ." Her voice trailed off as she thought about all the fun things she could do with the centerpieces.

I looked at Mom worriedly. I didn't think that working with Ashley and her mom was going to be fun at all. And I wasn't sure they'd be open to Mom's creative suggestions. I was fairly certain Ashley would ask for something super fancy and over-the-top. Not fun and quirky like Mom was famous for.

We'd find out soon enough. I was on store duty that day. Dad was supposed to fill in for me, but the night before he had realized he'd been driving with an expired license for a while now and had to make an emergency trip to the DMV. My sisters would have to go along with him. Day two of Camp Dad was off to an exciting start.

So my worst nightmare was coming true. I would actually have to help Ashley plan her birthday party. As a result, I had put a lot of thought into my work outfit that morning. I was going for cute, yet professional, and after much trial and error settled on white denim shorts, a sleeveless pink and white gingham shirt and pink ballet flats. I twisted my hair into two pigtail buns. Supercute, if I do say so myself. I checked my reflection out in the flower cooler and gave myself a nod of approval.

We had two appointments that day. The McGillicuddys would be coming in at noon. After they left, we'd have time to wolf down a quick lunch and then Ashley and her mom would be in at two o'clock.

At five to twelve the McGillicuddys arrived. They had

both been in the store before and I recognized them as soon as they walked in. Mrs. McGillicuddy was a short, older woman and he was equally small and elderly. She had close-cropped, snow-white hair that made her look like a cute little elf and blue eyes that crinkled around the edges when she smiled, which was a lot. Her husband was bald and wore these funny, black-rimmed glasses.

"Welcome to Petal Pushers, Mr. and Mrs. McGillicuddy!" Mom said warmly. "You remember my daughter Del?"

"Of course," said Mrs. McGillicuddy.

"Please, call us Geraldine and Jerome," insisted Mr. McGillicuddy.

"We're excited to plan our anniversary party," Mrs. McGillicuddy said, giving her husband's arm a gentle squeeze.

"Our fiftieth, can you believe it?" he said, patting her hand. "Imagine, she changed her last name from Smith to McGillicuddy just for me. If that isn't love, I don't know what is."

"Oh, Jerome," Mrs. McGillicuddy said with a laugh, though I'm sure she'd heard that one a thousand times. I couldn't help grinning as I showed them to the table.

But being around them made me a little sad, too. It made me miss my grandparents even more.

"And how are your parents doing down in Florida?" Mrs. McGillicuddy asked my mom, as if she were reading my mind.

As Mom filled them in on Gran and Gramps's latest adventures, I took a closer look at Geraldine and Jerome. Fifty years! They sat close to each other and finished each other's sentences and made each other smile. They certainly had a lot to celebrate. I also wondered what these harmless-looking people had done to incur the wrath of Great-aunt Lily. Perhaps appearances were deceiving.

As Mom took down the details of the party — in their backyard, under a tent, a catered lunch, fifty people (including their five kids, their spouses, and fifteen grandchildren). She determined that they needed five centerpieces, plus a large arrangement for the refreshment table.

"And what kind of arrangements are you thinking of? High? Low? Simple? Fancy?" Mom asked them.

"Maybe low arrangements, on the simple side," said Mrs. McGillicuddy slowly. Her husband nodded in agreement.

"And do you know what kind of flowers you like?" Mom asked. "Or would you like to take a look in the cooler and pick out some favorites?"

Mrs. McGillicuddy looked a little bashful. "Well, I love pink roses. They were the first flowers Jerome ever gave to me."

He smiled at the memory. "It was at the homecoming dance," he said. "You wore a white dress and your hair was up."

Mom and I exchanged glances. Mr. McGillicuddy certainly had a good memory!

He confirmed that with his next statement. "And you carried dahlias in your wedding bouquet."

She gave him a surprised look. "You remembered!"

"Of course!" he said.

"And when Charles was born you gave me a big bouquet of lisianthus," she said. She looked at us. "Our first child," she explained.

He nodded. "And we had the loveliest hydrangea bush in the backyard of our first house. . . ."

Mom was scribbling notes down quickly. She looked up. "You've given me some wonderful flowers to work

71

with," she said. "And I just love that each one says something about your lives together."

Suddenly, I had an idea. "Hey!" I said. "What if we print up a special document that explains the meaning of each flower to your lives? We could put it in a beautiful frame and put it on a display table."

Mrs. McGillicuddy beamed at me. "That's a great idea!" she said.

Mom nodded approvingly, and I felt a flush of pride.

Mr. McGillicuddy raised a hand. "Just in case you need any extra flowers to fill out the centerpieces, I think you should know that there's one flower we don't like at all. . . ."

"They're these white-and-pink lilies that are very . . . um . . . fragrant," Mrs. McGillicuddy said, clearly not wanting to offend Mom in case they were her personal favorites.

"You mean stargazers," said Mom. "Can't stand 'em myself. Fragrant is a nice word for it. They stink!"

"And they're dangerous, too," I piped up, remembering one of the many pieces of flower trivia I'd learned from Gramps and Gran. "You have to remove the pollen as the flowers start to open. If any of it gets on your clothes, it totally stains them a hideous shade of orange."

"No stargazer lilies," Mom wrote down. She looked up and smiled at the McGillicuddys. "It just happens that all the other flowers you've mentioned will look gorgeous together. We're going to make sure you have a simply lovely anniversary party."

Mr. and Mrs. McGillicuddy stood to leave. They were shaking hands with me and Mom and exchanging thank-yous when the bell over the front door rang.

I stood to greet the customer. "Welcome to Petal —"

"Hello, Delphinium," Aunt Lily said coolly. "I'm on my way to Kitty Dalrymple's garden tea and I thought I would bring her a bouquet of . . ." Her voice trailed off as she noticed our customers. "Oh, excuse me," she said. "Hello, Geraldine, Jerome," she said coolly.

"Hello, Lily," said Mrs. McGillicuddy in a grim tone. I stared at her. The sweet tone and smiling face were gone. Mrs. McGillicuddy was not looking very friendly at all.

"How have you been?" Mr. McGillicuddy asked Aunt Lily.

"Fine, thank you," replied Aunt Lily. "I hear congratulations are in order. For your golden anniversary."

"Thank you, Lily," said Mrs. McGillicuddy stiffly.

"We're looking forward to the party," Mr. McGillicuddy said, and his wife gave him a quick look, as if to remind him that Aunt Lily was *not* invited.

Aunt Lily seemed very uncomfortable. She pulled her ancient but gleaming alligator purse closer to her and turned away. "I'll just wait over here until you're ready," she said quietly to my mom.

I stared at Aunt Lily's retreating back. I knew exactly how she felt, being left out of a big party. But it was totally weird, feeling bad for my frosty great-aunt.

After the McGillicuddys left, neither Mom nor Aunt Lily said anything about the incident. Aunt Lily got her bouquet and left, and then I ran down to the Corner Café to pick up a couple of sandwiches before the Evil Edwardses arrived.

To be fair, Ashley's mom really isn't all that bad. She only raised the thorn in my side that is Ashley, no big deal, right? But Mrs. Edwards and my mom get along just fine. Plus, I was fairly certain Ashley wasn't any nicer to her

mom than she was to me, so I kind of felt sorry for her.
My stomach was so full of dread I could barely finish my
sandwich.

When I heard the bell jangle, I looked up and took
a deep breath to steady my nerves. As Ashley and her
mom walked inside, I heard Ashley say, "Just let me do the
talking."

Ashley wore a beaded, pale-yellow and green sarong
skirt, green tank top, and dangly earrings with multicolored stones. Metallic sandals laced up her legs. It was more
an outfit for a tropical vacation than downtown New
Hampshire. But even I had to admit she looked good. I
thought about how much time I had put into choosing *my*
outfit and laughed to myself. Foiled again!

I gave the two of them my best professional smile.
Ashley ignored me, but Mrs. Edwards gave me a quick
hug, leaving me smelling like fragrant French perfume.

"So nice to see you, Del," Mrs. Edwards said. She
turned to Mom and air kissed her. "Daisy! Our little girls
are turning thirteen! Can you believe it?" I rolled my eyes
at the "little girls" part, but stopped as soon as I realized
Ashley was doing the same thing.

Mrs. Edwards tugged at the hem of her short, crisp, white tennis dress as she sat in the chair Mom offered her. Her hair was an expensive-looking shade of blonde, held back with a pink headband. She wore a ring with a large diamond on her left hand. I knew she was about the same age as my mom, but looked a bit older because of all the time she spent in the sun, playing tennis and golf. Rumor had it that she had had some Botox injections to appear youthful, so I hoped she might frown so I could see if her forehead creased. Perhaps I could say something perplexing before the meeting was through. Mrs. Edwards smiled down at her attire. "Excuse my tennis whites," she said. "But I've got a four o'clock court time!"

For a second I thought she was going to dispute a parking ticket. Or maybe she had been caught jaywalking. Then I realized what she meant. Silly me. The Blooms are so not the Country Club types!

"So tell us about your event," Mom said, her purple pen poised above her notebook. "Is it at the Country Club?"

"No way," said Ashley snottily. "That's for weddings and anniversary parties. Lame. My party is going to be at Society Sisters!"

I clenched and unclenched my fists. I hated how rude Ashley was being to my mom and I hated how her mom was letting her get away with it. But mostly I hated sitting there listening to Ashley plan her stupid party that was ruining *my* actual birthday.

Mom let it all roll off her back. "Is that the new place on Old Country Road?" she asked pleasantly.

"Yes," said Ashley proudly. "And my party is going to be their very first event."

Mom bit her lip, unsure how to phrase what she had to say. "Sometimes with new venues, it isn't the best idea to be the very first party," she said carefully. "They need time to iron out the kinks. . . ."

Mrs. Edwards leaned toward Ashley. "Honey, she does have a point," she said. "Maybe we could consider another place before we give them the down payment. . . ."

But Ashley held up a hand. I glanced over to Mrs. Edwards to see if she was perturbed by her daughter's rude behavior, but her forehead was wrinkle free. "They've assured us that the party will be perfect," Ashley said smugly. "I'm not worried."

Mom gave a tiny shrug. "All righty then. Let's talk about the theme."

Ashley smiled. "One Thousand and One Nights," she said dreamily. "With jewel tones for the tablecloths and linens, brass genie lamps on the tables, burning incense. We'll eat sitting on the floor, surrounded by luxurious pillows. The lighting will be dim with flickering candles everywhere. . . ."

I couldn't help smiling. Exactly as I had suspected — over the top and totally inappropriate to the season. But I was glad she had the whole thing planned out. At least I didn't have to help her come up with ideas for her dumb party. Thank goodness for small favors.

Mom frowned. "So your party is going to be inside in the dark on what will probably be a gorgeous summer evening?"

Ashley looked crossly at Mom.

"I was thinking the same thing," said Mrs. Edwards. "Wouldn't a poolside party at the Country Club be more fun?"

"Mom!" Ashley shouted. "I've got it all figured out. And it's MY birthday. Will you PLEASE butt out?"

Mrs. Edwards sighed and shook her head. She gave Mom a look. "Well, it isn't every day a girl turns thirteen." She patted Ashley's hand. "You can have whatever you want, dear."

Mrs. Edwards looked over at me as if seeing me for the first time. "Hey, Del, isn't your birthday coming up, too? What are you doing for your big day?"

Working two stupid parties, I wanted to say. Instead, I answered, "We're going on vacation to Maine."

"Oh!" Mrs. Edwards said, clearly not impressed. "Well, won't that be fun for you."

Mom steered the conversation back to the subject at hand. "So I gather we're talking exotics," she guessed. "I have some fun thoughts to share. We could do blood lilies and hanging amaranthus with . . ."

Ashley shook her head. "I already know exactly what I want." She reached into her large, white studded leather bag and pulled out a sheaf of pages. They were each taken from a different glossy magazine. She rifled through them until she found the page she was looking for. She placed it on the table and tapped it with one pale pink–manicured fingernail. "This is from the latest celebrity party at

Chateau Marmont" — she looked at my mom — "a very fancy Hollywood hotel that all the stars go to," she explained as if Mom actually cared. "I want you to copy this exactly — studded golden vases with golden foliage, gold branches with crystals hanging from them, and chocolate artichokes."

I stared at the garish arrangement. It was a far cry from the mason jars filled with wildflowers that I coveted.

"How pretty," said Mom, although I was sure she didn't really think so. "But do you think it's a little dark for a summer . . ."

"These. Are. My. Centerpieces," Ashley said firmly.

Mrs. Edwards laughed nervously. "My Ashley knows what she wants!" she said.

If Mom was disappointed she wasn't getting a chance to be creative, she didn't show it. "I know the best place to order the flowers and the branches and foliage. But the crystals and the vases are going to be pricey." She glanced at Mrs. Edwards for approval.

Mrs. Edwards waved a hand. "Whatever it takes. I'll never hear the end of it otherwise."

Ashley turned to her mother. "Thanks, Mom,"

she said sweetly. She was getting exactly what she wanted and *now* she could afford to be nice. As much as I disliked Ashley, I couldn't help feel the tiniest bit of admiration for her. *She* would never be stuck working on her birthday!

Mom told them that she'd make some calls and present them with an estimate later in the week. Then we'd have to finalize the order one week in advance to be certain we'd get exactly what they wanted.

Before she left, Ashley turned to me with a sly grin, jangling an earring in her hand. "The RSVPs have been flooding in," she said. "No one wants to miss the party of the year." She wrinkled her nose as if she was thinking. "Can you guess who just confirmed that he's coming?"

I was pretty sure that I could guess who it was. But I simply shrugged as if I cared so little I couldn't even be bothered to speak.

"Hamilton Baldwin," she said.

Even though I had been prepared to hear his name, it still sent a little wave of shock through me. "And he asked if he could bring a guest." She bit her lower lip. "Wonder who that could be?"

Chapter Six

"The night is dark
in the park.
I walk
after dark.
It is dark dark dark."

Mom and I had just come home from the store when Poppy had steered us into the living room to join the rest of the family. She now stood in front of us "reading" from a notebook. Her hair was wet from her evening bath and you could see the comb marks in it. Instead of her usual pajamas, she was wearing an old black T-shirt of mine that fell below her knees. She finished and looked at us all expectantly. "The end," she said, giving us a look. I started clapping, and the others joined in after a moment.

The rest of my family looked puzzled, but I was pretty sure I knew what was going on with my little sister. I decided to confirm it.

"Nice poem, Poppy," I said.

She nodded.

"And how was your day?" I asked.

"Fine," my normally talkative sister said.

"Where did you go?" I asked.

"Water park."

The water park is Poppy's favorite place in the world. Any other day she'd be gushing for twenty minutes about the water slides, the lines, and the concessions. But not today.

Aster stared at Poppy, realization dawning in her eyes. She turned to me.

"I'm getting a bad feeling," Aster said softly. "Or am I imagining this?"

I shook my head. "No, it's just what you think."

Dark clothes. Dark poetry. Strangely silent. Poppy was acting just like Aster. And Aster didn't like it one bit.

"But why?" Aster asked me.

I shook my head. "Why does Poppy do anything?"

Aster looked at me blankly.

"Because she feels like it. It will pass."

Aster scowled. "I want it to pass *now*. How do I make her stop?"

I shook my head. "Your guess is as good as mine."

Aster looked annoyed, but I was amused. And it was nice to have something to take my mind off the comment that Ashley had made about Hamilton. Why would he bring a guest to her party? And who could it be? I was obsessing over it nonstop.

Dad felt so bad about his Ashley birthday mess-up that he gave me the next couple of days off, and he worked in the store. Well, I wasn't exactly off, since I had three little sisters to keep an eye on. But I managed to squeeze in a quick last visit with Heather and Amy before they went off on their summer trips, which was really nice. And I even enjoyed hanging out with my sisters; I found it pretty funny to see how Poppy's Aster act, all silent and broody, made my goth sister crazy.

"It's cute," said Rose. "I don't see why it bothers you so much."

As we sat around the kitchen table one morning finishing our bagels, Aster was seized with a sudden inspiration.

"Hey, Poppy," she said.

Silently, Poppy turned to her sister and raised an eyebrow. I nearly choked. Classic Aster move.

"I notice that your bedroom is yellow," she said. "Have you ever taken a look at the walls on my side of the room Rose and I share?"

I could see Poppy gulp.

"What color are they?" Aster asked.

"Black," Poppy said softly.

"I would never have yellow walls, Pops," Aster said. "Too sunshiny for me."

Poppy nodded. She got it.

The day was supposed to get pretty warm, so I decided we would head to the town pool. They offered free swimming lessons on Tuesdays and I could relax while my sisters swam. Plus, Poppy still loved to splash around in the kiddie pool. I wondered if I'd see anyone from school.

I showed our family pool card to the bored high school student behind the front entrance and we walked inside.

There were three pools — a deep pool with diving boards, a swimming pool with a section of cordoned-off lap lanes, and a kiddie pool. I waved to Carmine Belloni, Penelope Peterson, Chloe Davis, and Mike Hurley, who were playing Marco Polo in the main pool.

My sisters and I laid our towels down on the white plastic chairs near the big pool and slathered one another with sunscreen, paying special attention to super-pale Aster. Then I walked my sisters over to the big pool for their lesson and sat on the edge, my feet in the water, to watch. Poppy's group was blowing bubbles in the shallow end and doing the doggie paddle. I watched as Rose, Aster, and two other kids their age each lined up in a lane to determine their swimming ability. Rose was wearing a bathing suit with a big red strawberry on it and a ruffly skirt while Aster had on a black suit with a grinning purple skull. Typical.

I watched as my sisters dove in the water. Though they hadn't swum since last summer, Rose and Aster left the other kids in their wake. They reached out to touch the wall simultaneously, looked up, saw each other, and slapped hands. I shook my head. Completely different, yet so many similarities.

Sometimes Rose and Aster's closeness makes me feel a little left out. That's where Becky came in. Except, of course, when she was going away for the entire summer!

Enough thinking about that. The sun was beating down on me and I was ready to go for a swim myself. I decided to ease myself into the water instead of jumping in, which is never easy. The water was so cold I had to force myself to duck my head underneath. Finally my body began to adjust and I bobbed around for a while.

"Marco!" shouted Mike. I ducked out of the way of his flailing arms.

"Polo!" cried Carmine. "Hey, Del, wanna play?" he asked as he swam past me.

I shook my head no, swam over to the ladder, and climbed out. I was pretty good at diving and thought I'd practice a bit. It was fun bouncing off the low board and jackknifing cleanly into the water. After my sixth dive, I climbed out, dripping on the cement, and eyed the high board warily.

"Do it! Do it!" cried Rose and Aster from the side of the pool, egging me on. I closed my eyes. The high board both thrilled and terrified me, but I had never gotten up the nerve to try it. Then a voice in my head said: *Do it Del, do it before your birthday. That way you can always say, I dove off the high board when I was twelve.*

I liked the thought of that, and before I knew what I was doing, I was climbing up the steep ladder. My knees felt a little shaky as I walked to the end. The board wobbled. What was I thinking? But now that I was up there, there was no turning back.

I could see Rose and Aster pointing up at me, and Poppy, who had climbed out of the pool to get a closer look, jumping up and down. There was only one way out of this — I had to jump. At the very last moment I switched it to a dive. I put my hands together over my head, bent my knees, and sprung.

Splash! I hit the water pretty cleanly. I surfaced and swam to the ladder and climbed out, a big smile on my face.

"Yay, Del!" shouted Poppy. "You're so brave!"

Rose and Aster cheered.

I toweled myself off. I had done it. I just wasn't sure I ever wanted to do it again.

"Del! Del! Look at me!" Poppy cried. I turned around to see her setting off from one side of the pool. She doggie-paddled hard, sending up plumes of water, her face screwed up in concentration. I was poised to jump in if she needed help. But she miraculously made it to the other side without going under.

"That was great, Poppy!" I cheered, pulling her out and wrapping her in a big, striped towel. Poppy grinned, making it totally clear that she had dropped the Aster routine. She sat down on a chair and gave me her patented puppy-dog eyes. "Will you come into the kiddie pool with me?" she begged.

I wanted to say no, of course. But when your kid sister looks at you with those big, brown eyes and begs you to do something, even if it will be embarrassing, you kind of have to say yes. So I did.

I was sitting in the kiddie pool, surrounded by toddlers in their saggy swim diapers. *This water is probably fifty percent pee,* I thought to myself with a grimace. Poppy and I were making some "soup" and we each had a pail and shovel standing in as our pot and spoon. We were chopping pretend carrots. Apparently, I was slicing mine too big, so Poppy made me start over.

"Delphinium, is that you?" asked an extremely snotty voice.

I looked up just as Poppy decided to dump a bucketful of water over my head.

"Ha-ha, Del!" she cried. "I surprised you!"

I pushed my sopping hair out of my eyes and squinted into the sunlight to see who was talking to me. I could just make out the shape of a girl with long, straight brown hair. Correction — there were two of them. I shielded my eyes to take a closer look. It was Ashley's goons.

"Hello, Sabrina. Hello, Rachel," I said as dignified as possible under the circumstances — dripping wet, holding a plastic shovel as I sat cross-legged in the kiddie pool. I shook my head. "Why aren't you guys at the Country Club?"

"They're, like, repairing the pool," explained Sabrina.

"And where's your leader?" I asked.

Rachel scowled. "If you mean our *friend* Ashley, she's in Boston sampling cakes for her party," she said. "The one you're not invited to," she added unnecessarily. "But you *are* working there!" She and Sabrina laughed and slapped hands as if they had said something incredibly funny.

I ignored that. "And she let you two go out on your own?" I asked sweetly. "How nice of her."

Sabrina scowled and looked me up and down. "Nice suit," she said. "Think maybe it's time to, like, buy a new one?"

Puzzled, I glanced down at my bathing suit. I had bought it last year and thought it was supercute — a red-and-white-striped one-piece. But as I took a closer look I realized it was pretty faded from all the chlorine and the times I had forgotten it on the line for a day or two and left it to bake in the sun. I looked back up at Sabrina and Rachel. They were both in brightly colored string bikinis. Brand-new, I would guess.

"Yeah, good thing *Hamilton* didn't see you in it," offered Sabrina.

All thoughts of my old swimsuit left my head. "Hamilton was here?" I asked, showing perhaps a little too much interest.

The girls exchanged glances.

"You just missed him," explained Sabrina.

"He left in a big rush when that girl came to pick him up," finished Rachel.

When that girl *picked him up?* My heart skipped a beat.

"Anyone from school?" I asked in what I hoped was a very nonchalant voice.

Sabrina leaned forward, clearly relishing the moment. "No," she said dramatically. "An older woman."

Relief washed over me. "Oh, you mean a tall, blonde lady," I said. "That's his mom."

Rachel smiled wickedly and shook her head with a half smile, her eyes never leaving my face. "No, she was *definitely* not his mom. She actually looked just a couple of years older than us. Maybe in high school. Reallllly pretty."

"Oh," I said, my stomach sinking. Then I shook my head. I wouldn't let the Wonder Twins know they had rattled me. "Whatever," I said. "See you later." I returned to chopping pretend carrots.

"Much better," said Poppy approvingly.

Disappointed they weren't going to get a rise out of me, Sabrina and Rachel stomped off in their jeweled sandals.

But I couldn't help but stew. So *that* was why Hamilton had blown me off the other day! He obviously had a girlfriend. An older, attractive one at that. Then I remembered what Ashley had said. He was bringing a guest to her party. So the guest must be this pretty mystery girl.

My throat tightened. My summer was going from bad to worse. I thought about what Becky would say if she were there and decided to look on the bright side of things. *Good thing I'm not going to be anywhere near Ashley's party,* I thought. Dad had agreed that I would help Mom with the McGillicuddy's party and he'd step in to help Mom handle delivery and set-up for Ashley's.

So at least I wouldn't have to deal with the awkwardness of bumping into Hamilton and his girlfriend.

I straightened my shoulders, put on a fake smile, and dumped a bucket of water over Poppy's head. Her screams of delight improved my mood. For the moment at least.

❀   ❀   ❀

We spent the rest of the afternoon at the pool, swimming laps, diving off the low board (all of us except Poppy), and having fake tea parties at the bottom of the pool. Finally, sticky from chlorine and sunscreen and totally tired, we decided we had had enough. Poppy, who loved the water so much she had even suggested eating her chili dog in the kiddie pool, had the most shriveled up fingers and toes I had ever seen.

"They look like raisins!" she cried in delight. It was great to have Poppy — and not Poppy-channeling-Aster — back.

We toweled off, changed into our clothes, shoved our feet into our flip-flops, and headed to Petal Pushers to pick up Mom and Dad.

Ring-a-ling-ling. The air-conditioning in the store sent an icy blast to our wet heads.

Mom brightened as we walked inside. "My girls!" she cried. "How was your day at the pool?"

"We had a good time," I said, pushing the unpleasant moment with Sabrina and Rachel out of my head. "They all took a lesson. Poppy swam across the whole pool!"

"And Aster and I won a race," said Rose, her eyes glowing.

Aster nodded.

"Well, let me tell you," Poppy shouted, throwing her arms into the air. "It was amazing!" As we all watched, our mouths open, she burst into song. A show tune from the musical *Oklahoma!* to be precise:

"Oh, what a beautiful mornin'
Oh, what a beautiful day.
I've got a beautiful feeling
Everything's going my way."

Aster and I looked at each other. She shook her head in disbelief.

"What's up with Poppy?" Rose asked with a yawn. "She's being kind of annoying."

Chapter Seven

"Okay, let me get this down correctly," said Mom into the phone. "You want to double the amount of branches and crystals, add a rose petal and crystal garland, and change the chocolate artichokes to gardenias." She wrote down the information in her notebook. "You do know how expensive gardenias are, don't you?" She listened for a moment. "Okay, fine. No problem then. Yes, you can drop off the new magazine picture. Yes, I'll be sure to follow it exactly." She nodded. "Okay — I'll have a sample to show you tomorrow and we'll have to place the final flower order right afterward to get the flowers in time. See you then."

Mom hung up the phone and sighed. Apparently, an even more grandiose celebrity centerpiece had caught Ashley's eye, and she wanted Mom to copy that one instead.

"Luckily I have a few gardenia branches left over from Oscar's last order so I can do a sample arrangement," Mom said.

"It's Olivia all over again," I said. Olivia Post — Ashley's cousin, go figure — had been our demanding bridezilla client in the spring.

Mom nodded in agreement. "I think Ashley is *meshuga*," she said, tapping her index finger to her temple. I laughed as I heard the Yiddish word — which means "crazy" — come out of Mom's mouth. Mom is Catholic and Dad is Jewish, but they both had embraced each other's backgrounds completely.

"Well, if you think that's crazy, I heard that Ashley went down to Boston to sample special birthday cakes," I told her. "They apparently cost hundreds of dollars each."

"Whoa," said Mom. "Those Edwardses just like to throw their money away. As if we don't have the best bakery right here in town."

I nodded. Bella's Bakery had been around since my mom was little and their cakes are melt-in-your-mouth incredible.

"Well, if I ever have a birthday party," I said, "I would

serve Bella's strawberry shortcake for dessert." I smiled thinking about it. It was made with just-picked local berries and fresh cream. Mmmm-mmmm good.

Ring-a-ling-ling! The store bell chimed as the rest of the Bloom family made their entrance. Aster, in a black sundress, Rose in pink shorts and a white tank top and surprise, surprise, Poppy in a pair of pink shorts and a white tank top. I did a double take — Poppy's clothes were several sizes too big on her and I deduced that she had raided Rose's closet. Poppy apparently had not been able to locate a belt and had a piece of yarn looped around her waist, holding her shorts up rather precariously.

Rose, my somewhat self-centered sister, was completely clueless about her mini-me. Aster caught me staring at Poppy and gave me a small grin.

"You're just glad it isn't still you," I said.

Aster shrugged sheepishly.

"We came to pick you guys up!" Poppy squealed excitedly.

"Yeah," said Rose. "Dad took us to the Elwood Falls Historical Society today."

"How was it?" asked Mom.

"Educational," said Dad.

"Dusty," said Aster.

"Let's put it this way," said Rose. "Arrowheads. Pieces of old plows. Photos of people in funny-looking clothes. Big yawn."

"Yeah," called Poppy from the back of the store. "Big yawn."

"He took us to Von Schreiners afterward to make up for it," explained Rose.

Mom looked at the now-dancing Poppy worriedly. "Don't tell me. Big Rock Candy Mountain?" she asked. Poppy always orders this special sundae with gobs of candy stuck in it. She eats the entire thing and then can't sit still for hours.

Dad nodded and laughed sheepishly. Poppy was vibrating with energy. "Look at me! Look at me!" she shouted, hopping up and down. Then she decided to attempt a cartwheel. She put her hands on the floor, and kicked up her legs. Unfortunately, at that moment, the yarn holding up her pink shorts broke. So on her way down she realized she had to either stick her landing or grab her falling shorts. Wisely, she grabbed the shorts and was about to crash to the floor. I was the closest, so I lurched forward to grab her. But I was off-balance and we both landed in a heap on the floor. Luckily no one was hurt, so we just started laughing. The whole family joined in.

And that was, of course, when Great-aunt Lily walked in. She just stood there shaking her head. "Is this any way to run a business?" she asked.

Everyone stopped laughing and stared at me. Hmmf. That was usually *my* line. The similarities between me and mean old Aunt Lily were incredibly annoying.

The next morning, Mom and I were going to the store while Dad, Rose, Aster, and Rose 2.0 were going to the lake. I was a little envious. I love the lake: packing a picnic lunch, swimming out to the float and jumping off, holding my breath as I tried to touch the mucky bottom. But Mom needed my help. The McGillicuddys were coming in that morning to see their centerpiece before we placed the final order for the flowers. And that afternoon Ashley was coming for the same purpose. Ugh.

"But I trust you!" Mrs. McGillicuddy had said when Mom had called her to schedule the appointment. Still, we convinced her that it was a good idea to approve the centerpiece beforehand. Ashley had said no such thing. In fact, she had said, "It better look good!"

Mom was still shaking her head over that one. "That girl has no manners," she said as we finished up our quick breakfast.

"Tell me about it," I replied, putting my dish in the sink.

Poppy bounced down the stairs. Dressed all in pink, she sang out, "Twenty-two!" and stretched out her arms as if she was a Broadway star.

"Good morning, my love," Mom said. She looked at me. "What's up with Poppy?" she whispered to me.

"Poppy is Rose," I told her. "She used to be Aster."

Mom considered this. "Oh, okay" was all she said and took one last sip of her coffee. Nothing Poppy does ever fazes her.

At the store, I cleared off the worktable, and Mom placed Mrs. McGillicuddy's centerpiece on it first.

"Oh, Mom," I said. "It's beautiful!"

Mom had chosen antique-green hydrangeas to go with

the lisianthus, dahlias, and pink roses, which gave a real old-fashioned look to the arrangement. This classic look was enhanced by the vintage saltine cracker tin that was the vase. The centerpiece was simple, lovely, and home-spun, just like the McGillicuddys themselves. (Except, I remembered, when Aunt Lily was around.)

"I think the McGillicuddys are going to love it," I added.

Mom said, "I hope so," but she looked pleased.

Then Mom got a funny look on her face. "Now close your eyes," she said. I did. I could hear her slide open the cooler door and I heard a small grunt as she placed the heavy metal vase on the table. "Okay, open them."

I laughed out loud. Ashley's arrangement sat before me. The vase was heavy and awkward looking. Mom had spray-painted some branches gold and hung crystals from each one. She had also spray-painted some greenery the same garish color. The gardenias were beautiful, but totally overshadowed by all the shiny stuff and the rose petal and crystal garland. It was huge and ostentatious, especially compared with the charming McGillicuddy arrangement it dwarfed.

"That's going to take up the whole table," I chortled. "There won't be any room for dinner plates!"

Mom reached into her apron pocket and pulled out the magazine page Ashley had dropped off. I compared the two.

"But it matches exactly," I said with a shrug. *There is no accounting for taste,* I thought as I looked at the sweet, simple arrangement and the huge, imposing one. *To each his own* as Gramps always says.

Ugly flowers or not, I still felt a stab of envy as I thought about Ashley's elaborate birthday plans and how they were ruining my actual birthday. I wished I could talk to Becky about it. But her camp had a strict "no cell phone" policy and she was allowed one weekly call on the camp's lone pay phone. And I didn't feel like calling my other friends and explaining the whole story to them. My thoughts briefly went to Hamilton. But I hadn't heard from him since our awkward texting. Plus it seemed pretty clear he really did have a girlfriend. I felt totally alone.

Mrs. McGillicuddy was so happy with what Mom had done, she was speechless.

103

"Oh, thank you!" she finally said. "This is more beautiful than I even imagined." She touched each flower in turn. "So many memories . . ." she said softly. Mr. McGillicuddy looked pleased that his wife was so happy.

After the couple had left, Mom pulled out her notebook and wrote up the final orders. Mrs. McGillicuddy's was a snap. Mom had already picked up a slew of antique cracker, candy, and coffee tins in different shapes and sizes at the local flea market. Then she ordered the flowers all from the same supplier. "Done!" she said. "That was easy."

Ashley's order would not be so simple. If the little princess okayed the arrangement, the gardenias would have to be ordered from one place, the branches from a different one. And the crystals and the vases from yet another place. When Mom told me how much they were going to cost, I nearly choked.

But things were falling into place. Whether I liked it or not, we were ready for our two July 7 events. Not counting any unforeseen disasters. *But how often does that happen?* I thought.

You could tell that Ashley wanted to find something to criticize, but since the arrangement was exactly what she asked for, there was nothing she could say. But instead of thanking Mom, she simply said, "Now you're sure you can do ten of these just like this one?"

"I think she means to say thank you," said Mrs. Edwards, apparently trying to cover for her ungrateful daughter.

Ashley shrugged. "Thanks," she said with a total lack of sincerity.

I gave her a dirty look. She smirked back at me. "Jealous much, Delphinium?" she said snarkily.

I stared at the floor. She was right. I *was* jealous. But not that I wasn't invited — I had no desire to celebrate Ashley's thirteenth birthday. I realized I wished that it was *my* party.

Just then a cell phone began to ring a somewhat familiar tune. I leaned forward to hear better. It was an old '50s song — "It's My Party and I'll Cry if I Want To."

"So lame, Mom," said Ashley.

Mrs. Edwards laughed sheepishly and pulled the phone

from her Chanel bag. "Hello?" she answered. "Yes, this is she." She paused and frowned. "Wait, what are you saying?" Her face suddenly grew pale. Mom and I glanced at each other. Was everything okay? "I don't understand how this could happen!" Mrs. Edwards said angrily. "What kind of a business are you running?"

She held her hand over the phone and hissed to Ashley: "It's Society Sisters. They've double booked the night of your party."

Ashley's mouth fell open. "What?" she shrieked. "Are you kidding me? I don't get it!"

I get it, I wanted to say. *Your birthday has been ruined. Welcome to the club.* But wisely, I kept my mouth shut.

"They just realized they've booked a wedding there the same night." Mrs. Edwards explained. "And they are honoring their reservation, not ours."

Ashley's mouth opened and closed, but no sound came out.

I had never seen Ashley lose her cool like this. *See Ashley*, I thought, *sometimes things don't go exactly as you planned.*

"I'm going to have to call you back," Mrs. Edwards said

into the phone. "My daughter is freaking out. All thanks to you." She snapped her phone shut. "Oh baby, I'm so sorry," she said to the strangely silent Ashley. "They've offered to host your party in their barn instead and extend your party for an hour." Ashley just stared at her mom. "They use the barn for storage now, but they can clean it out. Maybe we could do a barbecue," she suggested. "That could be really fun," she said halfheartedly.

"But . . . but . . . I can't have a party in a barn!" Ashley wailed. "I was so excited about everything . . ." Ashley's voice trailed off and her lower lip trembled. Despite her expensive clothes and her perfectly glossed lips, she looked exactly the way she did in preschool on the day that her favorite stuffed rabbit, Mr. Wiggles, accidentally got run over by a pickup truck.

I felt a sudden rush of sympathy. So what if she was my sworn enemy and the meanest girl in school. She was disappointed. And if anyone knew how that felt — my friends gone, my birthday postponed, my crush having a girlfriend — it was me.

But feeling sorry for my biggest enemy was a weird sensation, that was for sure.

Chapter Eight

"I can't believe it," said Dad, stabbing the air with his fork, an asparagus spear drooping on either side. "Society Sisters booked two parties on the same day! What were they thinking?"

I gave him a look.

He had the grace to look chagrined. "I guess it happens," he said.

Mom laughed. "Yeah, I guess so!" She shook her head. "It's a shame to lose the business, though." She took a sip of water. "I warned Ashley it wasn't a good idea to have the first party at a new venue. They need some time to iron out the kinks."

"It sounded like such an incredible party," said Rose wistfully.

"Incredible," echoed Poppy, patting the jaunty pink headband with a pink bow she wore in her hair. Yes, she was still being Rose, and Rose *still* didn't seem to realize it.

"Well, you must be relieved, Del," said Aster.

I shook my head ruefully. "I thought I would be," I said. "My birthday can be salvaged and my ex–best friend is getting her just deserts." I shrugged. "But for some reason I just feel bad for her. And for us, for losing the business, of course." I smiled grimly. "After all, I know what it's like to be disappointed on your birthday."

I saw Mom and Dad exchange a sappy glance. "Del, that's really mature of you," Dad said.

"Don't give me too much credit," I said. "It's mostly because we need the business. We have to keep things going for Gran and Gramps!"

I jumped as Buster pressed his cold nose into my bare leg, begging for a handout. "No more scraps for you, Buster," I said. "You're getting chubby." That didn't seem to faze him and he moved on to Aster.

"They did offer to move the party to the barn," mused Mom. "But I guess that isn't fancy enough for Ashley."

Dad got that look on his face when he's about to quote someone. "As Jonathan Swift once wrote, 'You can't make a silk purse out of a sow's ear,'" he said.

"Huh?" said Rose. "What does that mean?"

"Yeah, what does that mean?" Poppy repeated. Rose looked at her quizzically.

"It means you can't make something fancy out of something inferior," Dad explained. "Ashley can't turn a dirty barn into a fancy party space."

Dad has a lot of sayings, some I listen to and some that go in one ear and out the other. But for some reason, this one really stuck with me. That night after I fell asleep, I dreamt of old-fashioned ladies in fancy dresses holding pigs' ears as purses and big, fat, pink pigs with jeweled handbags for ears. I woke up, shaking my head. How weird.

I lay in bed, amusing myself with thoughts of Ashley, dressed in a gown and tiara, sitting on a hay bale at a gorgeously set table. Crystal chandeliers hung from the beams and the tables were covered in lace, with fine china, silver candlesticks, and platters of gourmet food.

I expected to give myself a good laugh. But then I received a surprise. In my mind's eye, the beautiful tables and decorations looked pretty amazing against the rustic setting.

I sat up straight in bed. Who said Ashley had to change her fancy party to a barbecue? She could have her totally over-the-top event in the barn! We could put Oriental carpets on the floor. Hang chandeliers, bring in gilt chairs, set the table with gorgeous linens and china and crystal and really go over the top. This would be way more amazing and one-of-a-kind than a party in a catering hall!

I slipped out of bed. I was the only one up. It was still really early, not even six o'clock. I hovered outside of Mom and Dad's room, listening intently for signs of life. I waited on pins and needles until I couldn't take it anymore. Then I crept into their room and stood over Mom, who was sleeping soundly, her arm thrown across her face. Dad was buried under the covers, snoring softly.

The power of my thoughts (or perhaps the fact that I poked her shoulder) must have woken Mom up.

"Del!" she said, slightly panicked, sitting up. "What's wrong?"

"Nothing," I whispered. "I just figured out how to save Ashley's party!"

That got her right up. Mom slipped out of bed and we headed downstairs. We settled on the living room couch. And then I told her my idea.

Mom grinned. "It *is* one of a kind," she said. "I bet she's going to love it." Then she frowned. "But what about the flowers?" she asked. "It's too late to order all the gardenias and crystals she wanted."

"One thing at a time, Mom," I said. "Let's focus on the setting first!"

We spoke with Society Sisters, who were more than happy to help us try to salvage the party they had lost. They gave us a list of all the decorations they had and we found the rest. We called antique shops, home decorating stores, and garden supply shops. We picked up chandeliers, gilt birdcages, and oil paintings in fancy golden frames. Aunt Lily even came through with an old Oriental rug that had been gathering dust in her attic. Society Sisters cleaned out that barn in record time and helped us decorate.

Mrs. Edwards agreed to bring Ashley to the barn at dusk that evening even if she had to drag her there. I got a good laugh just imagining that.

Mom and I met our guests in the parking lot. Mrs. Edwards looked hopeful and Ashley just looked grumpy.

"So I hear you're trying to save my party, Delphinium," she said sarcastically. "Well, don't waste your time. I'm only here because my mom forced me to come."

I said nothing and began to lead Ashley and her mom down the narrow brick walkway that led from the parking lot to the barn.

We had lined the path with luminarias. Mom and I had gotten fancy with plain brown paper bags and a hole puncher, creating a beautiful pattern. Then we filled the bottoms of the bags with sand and placed a candle in a glass votive inside each one.

When we reached the clearing in front of the barn, I paused. There was a tire swing near the entrance and we had covered the rope with a flowery vine. We had even decorated the rough wooden fence and benches nearby. It really was picture perfect. The barn door creaked loudly as I rolled it to the side. Ashley and her mom stared in silence at the glowing, glistening room. The floor was covered in several rich-looking Oriental rugs. Chandeliers, dripping with crystals, hung from the beams over the tables. In the corners were ornate birdcages. Mom, always thinking of every creative detail, had added colorful fake birds hanging out on the perches inside. We had set up one table completely, which was covered with glittering crystal, fine bone china, and fancy candlesticks. After much thought, we had gone with a square glass centerpiece lined with leaves and packed with white calla lilies. It was fun, totally funky, and completely unexpected. It was perfect. But would Ashley agree?

Mrs. Edwards clasped her hands together. "It's amazing."

Ashley looked around. "I just don't know," she said. "It's gorge, don't get me wrong. Really gorge," she admitted grudgingly. "But who throws a party in a barn? What if everyone thinks it's stupid?"

I groaned inwardly. Was all our hard work for nothing?

Just then Mom blurted out, "Well, *Jennifer Aniston* didn't think it was stupid when *she* had her fancy party in a barn!"

Huh? I turned to look at Mom. She wouldn't look at me. "I read it in *Us Weekly*!" she added.

Ashley considered this for a moment. Then she smiled. "Well, it is quite beautiful," she said thoughtfully. "And cutting edge, too." She nodded. "It's brill."

"So shall we do it?" asked her mother.

"Let's do it!" said Ashley. Then she was silent for a moment, eyeing the calla lilies. "The only thing that has to go is the flowers. I need something really special for my party. These centerpieces are lame."

Mom looked fed up. I wasn't upset, though. I was getting used to Ashley's obnoxious comments.

"Oh, don't worry!" I said, jumping right in. "These are just placeholders. We have something really amazing planned. You're just going to love it."

Ashley and her mom left the barn chattering excitedly. As soon as they were gone, Mom and I simultaneously let out a deep breath and collapsed into two of the golden bamboo chairs with silk, off-white cushions. I bounced on my seat. They were pretty comfy.

We exchanged glances. "Jennifer Aniston?" I asked Mom with a grin. "You made that up, didn't you?"

She shrugged. "It *could* be true," she said.

" 'Something really amazing planned?' " she asked me.

I shrugged back. "We'll figure it out, Mom. We always do."

Chapter Nine

I needed a day off after all the drama, so Dad worked at the store the next day. He was going to take orders, greet customers, do simple arrangements, and only interrupt Mom if something big came up. She was concentrating on creating an amazing centerpiece for Ashley. The Edwardses were going to stop by on the Fourth of July to make the final decision. That was the next day. So the clock was ticking.

I for one was glad to be lazily hanging out at home with my sisters. I was flipping through the channels, and Poppy was playing Go Fish with Aster. Then Rose came down the stairs and stood in front of me.

"I'm bored," she announced. "Can we go to the mall?"

Apparently, there's only so much relaxation my sisters are capable of.

"Everyone up for it?" I asked, hoping someone would say no. These days the mall meant Fleur to me. What if I ran into Hamilton? How awkward would that be? Aster shrugged. Poppy was on board, of course.

I called the store to tell Mom and Dad where we were going. "Fine, fine," said Dad distractedly.

"How are the centerpieces coming along?" I asked him.

"Not so well," he said. "Your mom has tried seven different arrangements and she's starting to get . . . frustrated."

I grimaced. "She hasn't started saying she doesn't know why she ever thought she was good at flower arranging, has she?" I asked.

"Oh yeah," said Dad.

"Then you have my sympathy," I told him.

My sisters and I took the bus and soon we were walking through the mall's north entrance.

"Where should we start?" I asked. Rose and Poppy decided they wanted to look in the windows of the pet store first.

The puppies and kittens were adorable. Especially a

long-haired dachshund that put its paws on the window and looked at us with big, sad eyes and started to howl a little puppy howl. So of course Poppy had to go inside and ask if she could hold her. It took a while to convince our little sister it was time to go. "I need that puppy!" she cried. "She would be my best friend! Buster could be her big doggie brother!"

Next, we went to the hat shop and tried on almost every hat in the store. Rose put on the largest, floppiest hat I had ever seen and said, "After all, tomorrow is another day!" the closing line from our mother's favorite movie, *Gone with the Wind*. Poppy, not to be outdone, put on a fedora and tried a line from Dad's favorite movie, *Casablanca*, and got it all wrong: "Of all the gym joints in all of the world, she walks into mine," she said. We laughed and laughed until I caught the hat store lady glaring at us and I escorted everyone out.

For Aster, we paid a visit to the comic book store, but we got bored and had to eventually drag her away from the *Nightmare Before Christmas* collectibles. I made a mental note to buy her one for Christmas-slash-Hanukkah.

"I'm hungry!" said Rose.

"Me too," said Poppy.

So we headed to the food court. But I got mixed up and I didn't plan my route properly and to my dismay I realized we were about to pass Fleur.

"Hey!" said Poppy. "Isn't that where we were spiers?" she asked excitedly.

Back in May, I thought that Hamilton had stolen prom ideas from us and I had gone to Fleur to find out if it was true. Poppy ended up coming with me and we had had quite an adventure. I ignored the quizzical looks from Rose and Aster. I would explain later if I had to. First, I had to get past the place.

Don't look, don't look, don't look, don't look, I chanted to myself. But of course I did. And there, standing by the front counter, talking to his mom, was Hamilton Baldwin. Seeing him kind of took my breath away. He looked tan — more like a light shade of golden brown, to be exact — and he was wearing a baseball cap and shorts. He looked totally cute. My heart melted a little. It had been thirteen days since I had seen him. Not that I was keeping track or anything.

Then he stepped to the side and I saw her. The pretty, older girl that Rachel had told me about. I wasn't prepared for exactly how pretty and how much older she looked. She was at least fifteen, with long, straight, dark hair and big, dark eyes. She laughed and touched Hamilton's arm. And that's all I saw because then I had to turn away.

At the food court, my sisters loaded up on snacks, but I had no appetite. Aster looked at me worriedly when I turned down her offer of a piece of a soft pretzel, my favorite.

So Sabrina and Rachel had been right. Hamilton had a girlfriend. A beautiful, older girlfriend. And apparently, her parents didn't own a rival florist and she could show her face at Fleur whenever she wanted to.

I was done. I couldn't compete with that.

I woke up the next morning, the Fourth of July, the air already hot and heavy. The cicadas were humming. Usually, I love the weird sound they make, which reminds me of hot summer days gone by. But today it just irritated me. Hamilton had a girlfriend. We still hadn't figured out Ashley's centerpieces. Although I wasn't invited to the party of the year, I was somehow orchestrating the whole thing. And my birthday was going to be the worst birthday in the history of birthdays.

As Mom and I walked to work, the time and temperature provided for us by Elwood Falls Bank told us it was already eighty-seven degrees at 8:30 a.m. We were drenched by the time we got to the store. But we put on the air conditioner full blast and we were soon totally cool and comfortable. We had a steady stream of customers all morning, which was good because it distracted me from my woes. Whether it was that everyone had fallen in love with Mom's new jaunty red-white-and-blue Fourth of July corsages — no dyed carnations for her: instead she created a red gerbera daisy, white hydrangea sprig, and blue bachelor's button version — or that they just wanted to get out of the heat even for a few minutes, I wasn't sure. But we ran out of corsages by 11:30 a.m., and Mom had to start making more to keep up with the demand.

"So how are Ashley's centerpieces coming along?" I asked cautiously as I twisted floral wire around the flower stems. I knew Ashley and her mom were coming in later that day to see them and I hadn't had the nerve to ask Mom the night before.

Mom smiled and pushed a lock of hair behind her ear. "Believe it or not, I'm done," she said. "I have four arrangements I like. I think we'll be okay."

I took a peek in the cooler. The arrangements did look very pretty. *But are they special enough for Little Miss Persnickety?* I wondered.

By noon, my entire family was in the store. Our house is an old Victorian with what Dad calls "ancient wiring" and the only room that has air-conditioning is my parents' bedroom. We don't often need it, as the New Hampshire nights are generally pretty cool. But the house was crazy hot already, per Rose.

"Crazy!" shouted Poppy with an emphasis on the "azy."

So we spent the day in the store. Rose paced around doing singing exercises and generally driving everyone crazy. Poppy, of course, was pacing and singing right along with her. "Maaa, mooo, meee, mooo," she sang. When Aster and Dad got bored they would wander out to pick up Fourth of July delicacies like popcorn balls and lime rickeys and corn dogs, and come back to the store to share them with the rest of us in the A/C.

At quarter to one, Dad put down his paper and stood up. "It's almost time for the parade, girls," he said. "I wish it went down this street; I'd watch it from the front window instead of facing the heat!"

"We'll be right behind you guys," I said as Dad left with my sisters. Mom and I had agreed to close the store for an hour to watch the parade. But Ashley and her mom were running late and still hadn't arrived. Finally Mom sent me on my way. "No sense both of us missing the parade," she said. "I know how much you love it. I'll be there as soon as I can."

I nodded and pushed open the door. The heat hit me like a big, hot, wet, wool blanket. Yuck. The crowds were out in full force, but everyone looked pretty miserable. The only happy person I saw was Ed Heins, who was manning the Shaved Ices — 21 Delicious Flavors! booth. People were lined up down the block for the iced treats.

I spotted Dad, Poppy, and Aster, who luckily had found a spot in the town square under a shady tree. We watched as the high school marching band, sweat pouring down their faces, marched down the street playing "Stars and Stripes Forever." One of the majorettes dropped her baton and looked like she was considering leaving it behind and going home. She finally picked it up and halfheartedly marched on.

All the little kids dressed in their finest red-white-and-blue outfits were dragging their feet. One little guy sat down on the curb right in front of us and refused to go on. The kids on their tricycles, who usually zipped down the street in excitement, had to be pushed by their parents. There was no breeze and the red-white-and-blue ribbons from their trike handles hung limply.

Finally, the floats appeared. Little George Washington looked like he was going to keel over as he chopped down the cherry tree. The Statue of Liberty was fanning herself with the big book she carried. Betsy Ross sewed her flag rather halfheartedly, I noticed. And finally, the Uncle Sam float rolled down the street. He always brought up the rear of each parade, like Elwood Falls's version of Santa at the Macy's Thanksgiving Day Parade. He was tossing handfuls of candy to the now rapidly thinning crowd. I laughed out loud. Instead of his usual patriotic three-piece suit and star-spangled top hat, he was wearing red-white-and-blue swimming trunks. Genius.

When we returned to the store, we found Mom with a scowl on her face.

"I missed the parade for the first time in thirty-seven years," she said sadly. "Ashley was here for so long. She hated all the centerpieces. I don't know what we're going to do."

"She hated them?" Dad cried, his face falling.

I gulped. We had saved the party — but what were we going to do about the flowers? Gran and Gramps had taught me that the customer was always right. But everything about Ashley was just so very wrong.

As the day went on, my family and I tried tossing around ideas for Ashley's centerpieces, but nobody came up with anything we could use. We sent Dad and Aster out for root-beer floats, but even those didn't inspire us. The customers had stopped coming in, so we sat around the table dejectedly slurping our drinks.

Rose glanced idly at the wall clock. "Yikes!" she yelled. "I've got to go!" She grabbed the bulging plastic bag she had hauled to the store with her and disappeared into the back room.

"Holy petticoats!" said Aster as Rose emerged from the back. She looked miserable in a long, old-fashioned dress, a stiff-looking bonnet, and pantaloons.

Mom gasped. "Oh, Rose," she said. "You look so uncomfortable."

Dad shook his head. "It's way too hot out for that getup."

Rose straightened her bonnet. "The show must go on," she said.

Poppy stared at her. She nodded. "The show is on," she echoed.

Rose gave her a funny look. Then she shrugged. "See you afterward, for the fireworks!" she said, giving us a deep curtsy.

"Break a leg, Rose!" called Mom.

We closed up the store, collected our picnic basket and blanket, and made our way to the baseball field for the pre-fireworks show. It started with a "funny" skit with one-liners from the Founding Fathers. George Washington and Betsy Ross sang a duet. There was a short play dramatizing the signing of the Declaration of

Independence. And finally, our Rose, singing "America the Beautiful."

The crowd had been buzzing during the rest of the show. But a silence fell over everyone as Rose began to sing. She really does have a lovely, clear voice. And believe me when I tell you, she really belted that song out. By the time she got to the end: "From sea to shining seaaaaa!" the crowd was on its feet.

"Hooray for Rose!" I yelled.

"Bravo!" shouted Dad.

"That's my girl!" Mom cheered proudly.

Rose's face was bright red under her bonnet. You could tell she was dripping with sweat, even from where we were sitting. But she had a big smile on her face as she waved to the crowd and curtsied.

I turned to Poppy. "So will that be you onstage someday?"

She looked me in the eye. "No way, José," she said, removing her pink headband. "That didn't look like fun at all!"

I guessed her Rose Period was over. Who knew what would come next?

It was just too hot to move. So we lay down on the blanket and sweated in silence as we waited for the fireworks to begin. Rose soon joined us, her face glowing with a combination of perspiration and excitement. We congratulated her on her performance, then opened the picnic basket, filled with fried chicken and potato salad. But we just picked at our food. It was just too hot to eat.

Finally, the sun went down and the fireworks began. Our town goes all out for the Fourth of July fireworks. They are really big, really colorful, and really, *really* loud.

I love them all, but if I had to choose I'd have to pick those white ones that glimmer as they trail down, kind of like the branches of a giant, weeping willow tree. I watched, entranced, as the sky lit up with a multicolored torrent of flashes, sparkles, corkscrews, and bursts — the pops, bangs, crackles, and sizzles reverberating in my ears.

I noticed that the crowd seemed to like these new fireworks that exploded into round, colorful smiley faces and peace signs, but they didn't really do it for me. I'm a fireworks traditionalist, I suppose.

As always, Dad shook his head. "I remember when I was little, in 1976, I saw an American flag, made entirely of fireworks," he said.

"Sure, Dad," we said, like we always do.

Then it was time for the finale. A relentless and spectacular barrage of colorful explosions, with the *boom-boom* booming deep in the pit of my stomach. And then finally, regretfully, it was over.

The air was thick with smoke and smelled of sulfur. I thought about the glowing lights, the shimmering sky, and the patriotic reds, whites, and blues.

As the smoke cleared, I grabbed Mom's arm.

"I have a totally awesome idea for Ashley's centerpieces!" I cried.

Chapter Ten

The next morning at breakfast, Dad looked up from the paper. "It was a hundred and one degrees yesterday, can you believe it? One of the majorettes had to be taken to the hospital for heat exhaustion!" he reported. "But sales of concessions were way up this year."

"We sold a lot of corsages," Mom offered.

"There isn't an air conditioner or fan to be bought in the area," he said. "And today's going to be just as bad." He thought for a moment. "Girls, shall we go to the lake or the water park today?"

"Movies!" cried Poppy.

Last night had been unbearable and, one by one, my sleepless sisters and I had dragged our blankets and pillows to camp out on Mom and Dad's floor. When Mom woke up and saw us she had laughed. "I'm surrounded by Blooms!" she had said.

Today, Mom and I would be putting together the centerpieces for both parties. When Mom called Mrs. Edwards with my idea for the flowers to run by Ashley she had simply said, "Just go for it." I guess she couldn't stomach the thought of yet another centerpiece viewing. Neither could we. So we were going for it. I felt confident that even Ashley wouldn't be able to have anything bad to say about these arrangements. Or at least I hoped so.

The store was nice and quiet after the craziness of the previous day. I was looking forward to spending some time cleaning and organizing. So I was more than a little disappointed when my whole family piled into the store shortly after we arrived.

"The movie doesn't start till noon," Dad explained. "And it's just too hot in the house."

So I put everyone to work. I handed Rose the broom, Poppy and Dad each got a feather duster, and I sent Aster into the cooler.

"Thanks, Del!" she said sincerely.

I headed over to the phone and started listening to the messages when Poppy's voice broke the silence.

"Here, let me show you how to do that," she said impatiently, dropping her feather duster and heading over to Rose. "Give it to me." She grabbed the broom. It was way too big for her and she nearly fell over. "Really, Rosie. You don't just move the dust around. You make piles!"

I realized everyone was staring at me.

"Why are you being so bossy, Poppy?" I asked. Then I took a closer look at my sister. She was wearing a green T-shirt and denim skirt. I was wearing a green T-shirt and denim skirt. And she had a pair of sunglasses on top of her head, holding back her hair. I raised my hand to my head. I had a pair of sunglasses on top of my head!

"Poppy, are you being . . . me?" I asked.

Poppy nodded.

"Well, I am not that bossy!" I spluttered.

Poppy nodded enthusiastically. "Oh yes, you are!" she said.

Rose snorted and Aster hid her smile behind her hand. I ignored them.

Finally, it was time for Dad and the girls to go to the movies. I went into the back of the store so I could work on Ashley's centerpiece in private. I wanted to surprise Mom. I hadn't been quite sure how to pull it off, so I'd had to consult the Internet. But I was pretty sure I had figured it all out.

When I was finished, I waited until Mom was busy in the cooler. Then I brought my arrangement to the worktable and turned out the lights.

Mom stepped out of the cooler, a bucket of roses in her hands. She gasped when she saw the arrangement. "It's so . . . it's so . . ."

"Amazing?" I offered.

"Amazing," she agreed. "And innovative." She looked at me again and a big smile spread scross her face. "And really cool!" She gave me a squeeze. "Del, I think you did it!"

The rest of the day was business as usual. Then later that afternoon, Dad came in, leading Poppy by the hand.

"The twins discovered that they outgrew their water shoes and need to go shopping before we go to Maine," he said. "But Poppy refuses to go to the mall. She keeps insisting on going to the pool."

I looked at Mom. She shrugged. "It's pretty dead in here," she said, and it was true — we hadn't had a single customer drop in while I worked on Ashley's centerpiece. "Tomorrow's going to be a late night," Mom added. "Del, why don't you leave early and take her?"

I shrugged. "All right," I said. Actually, a dip in the town pool would be pretty nice.

Dad took us home and waited while we got our swimsuits, some towels, and our family card that let us in. Then he dropped us off at the pool.

"See you later!" he called as he drove off.

"This was a good idea," I told Poppy as we approached the front desk. "I can't wait to jump in."

"Me neither!" Poppy said in a confident, grown-up-sounding voice. I gave her a look, but she just smiled sweetly at me.

As I anticipated, the pool was crowded. Poppy and I dropped off our clothes and towels on the lone free chair we could find, and headed over to the main pool. We swam for a while and I tried to teach Poppy how to do the dead man's float. She didn't like putting her face in the water, so I wasn't very successful.

Then I had to go to the ladies' room. I deposited Poppy on our white plastic lounger with strict instructions not to move.

When I came out of the bathroom, I noticed a big crowd gathered around the diving pool. *I wonder what's going on?* I thought. I took a quick detour to check things out. I frowned. Everyone was looking up at the high board and pointing to it.

I shielded my eyes and looked up, too. And there, to my disbelieving eyes, was my little sister, frozen in fear at the end of the board, high above the crowd. It looked like she was crying.

"Mother-of-pearl," I said, one of Gran's favorite fake swears. The lifeguard was standing at the top of the high board's ladder, trying to coax Poppy to come to him. But she wasn't moving.

I pushed through the crowd.

"Poppy, hang on!" I cried. I went to the bottom of the ladder and called up to the lifeguard. "Hey, I'm her sister! Maybe I should try," I said.

He shrugged and climbed down. He looked embarrassed. "I shouldn't have let her climb up," he said. "But she insisted she was brave and could do it."

With a gulp, I realized what was going on. Poppy was dressing like me, talking like me, bossing people around like me, and now she was jumping off the high board, just like me. Just like she had mimicked Aster and Rose before. But why was she doing this? I had to get to the bottom of her behavior.

But first, I had to get her off the high board in one piece.

I took a deep breath and climbed up the ladder, rung by rung. When I got to the top I stood at the far end so I wouldn't accidentally bounce my sister into the pool.

"Hey, Poppy!" I called out cheerfully, even though my heart was pounding mad fast. "Whatcha doing?" I was trying to be as casual as possible so I wouldn't freak her out anymore than she already was. But it was hard to keep my cool.

"Del, I'm scared!" she whimpered, not taking her eyes off the crystal blue water below.

"All you have to do is take a step backward," I said.

"Huh?"

"Just take one big step backward and we'll take it from there."

"O-okay." Poppy sniffled. She nodded and stepped backward. She almost lost her footing and the crowd gasped.

"You're fine, Poppy, you're fine," I assured her. "Now take one more."

She did it. "And now that you're away from the edge you can turn around and walk toward me."

Poppy shook her head. "I can't."

"Yes, you can, Poppy," I assured her. "Just face me. You can do it."

I saw her little shoulders shake. Then she took a deep breath and turned. Her eyes were as round as saucers.

"Great!" I said. "Now put your hands on the rails. Look me in the eyes and walk right toward me."

Poppy gripped the rails so hard her knuckles turned white. Then slowly, slowly, she took a step forward.

"That's great, Poppy!" I said encouragingly. "Now a couple more . . ."

A few seconds later, Poppy was clutching my leg for dear life. After I hugged her and then detached her, I helped her down the ladder. The crowd cheered when we got to the bottom. My legs nearly buckled when I was on solid ground and I realized I was drenched in sweat. That had taken a lot out of me. I had to walk over to our lounge chair, sit down, and take a deep breath. Poppy, of course, was as fine as could be.

"Wanna make soup?" she asked me.

I smiled weakly. "Sure," I said. Anything to stay on solid ground.

I decided to wait till the walk home to talk to Poppy. "So why did you climb to the top of the high board?" I asked.

"I wanted to be just like you, Del," she said matter-of-factly.

"First you were Aster."

Poppy nodded.

"And then you were Rose."

Poppy nodded again.

"And now you're me," I concluded. *Hey,* I realized, *why didn't she want to be* me *first?*

Poppy shook her head. "Not anymore," she said. "That high board was too scary!"

Well, at least that was taken care of. "But why have you been acting like us all week?" I said. "You're not Aster, or Rose, or me. You're Poppy, and we like you just the way you are."

Poppy looked down at the ground. "You want to be a florist. Aster wants to be a poet. Rose wants to be an actress. You all know what you want to be."

Realization dawned on me. "Does this have to do with your graduation?" I asked.

She nodded, her eyes still downcast. "I don't know what I want to be when I grow up."

"Oh, Poppy," I said. "Nobody really knows. I could end up being a doctor. Aster could be a chef. Rose could be a librarian." I smiled at her. "There's so much time for you — and all of us — to decide. Just because we like something now doesn't mean we have to do it for the rest of our lives!"

Poppy raised her eyes and considered this.

"And you are your own person, Pops," I said. "You don't need to pretend to be any of us. You're different, and that's good."

She gave me a dubious look.

"I don't know anyone else who counts the same set of stairs every morning," I said. "Who wears two different colored socks almost every day. Who could go two weeks only eating foods that start with the letter *L*."

Poppy still looked skeptical.

"That was a lot of lettuce and lentils," I reminded her. I thought of something else. "And who makes up her own words," I added. "Face it, Pops. You are creative and entertaining, and you're really funny!"

Poppy had a very thoughtful look on her face. I smiled, confident that I had gotten through to her.

"You're right, Del," she said. "I am funny." Then she threw her arms in the air. "That's it! I know what I want to be when I grow up. A clown!" I laughed, and she smiled at me. "I feel so . . ."

"Pondiferous?" I guessed.

She rolled her eyes. "No . . . intervisable," she said. At my blank look, she explained. "It means relieved."

I sighed. Poppy hadn't *really* gotten my message. But at least she wouldn't be climbing the high board anymore. That made me feel *intervisable*, too, that was for sure.

I woke up early the next day and started packing. Tomorrow — my birthday — would be crazy busy and we wanted to leave for Maine first thing in the morning on Sunday. I carefully folded T-shirts, bathing suits, underwear, socks, jeans, and sweatshirts and placed them in my suitcase along with sandals, sunglasses, water shoes, and four — no, make that five, to be safe — paperbacks I couldn't wait to read. I also added a brand-new sundress that I planned to wear to my birthday dinner at Brown's.

It had taken a while, but I was feeling okay with how things were turning out for my birthday. I'd be doing the things I loved most — arranging flowers and helping out the family business. It still annoyed me that I was giving Ashley an amazing party while I'd be celebrating on a much smaller scale, one day late. But it was what it was.

Mom and I were running late and had to practically sprint to the store to open in time. I had just stepped behind the counter when two older women walked in.

"I'd like a dozen roses," said the woman with the bluish-white hair.

"Red, white, yellow, or pink?" I asked, indicating the vases in the cooler behind me.

She looked at them all. "Oh, it's so hard," she said. "Maybe a mix?"

As I wrapped them up in crackly cellophane, I eavesdropped on their conversation. "So what are your plans for this weekend?" the blue-haired lady asked her friend, who had a snow-white bob.

"George and I are going to the McGillicuddys' anniversary party tomorrow," said the lady with the bob.

"Oh, how lovely," said the blue-haired lady. "Is it their golden anniversary?" she asked.

"It is! Their kids are coming in from all over the country. It's going to be a wonderful party."

I stared at them. Dare I ask? Finally, I realized I wouldn't be able to live with myself if I didn't.

I took a deep breath. "I hate to bother you," I said once

I had stapled the bouquet closed and beribboned it. "But I was wondering if you knew why Lily Hastings and Geraldine McGillicuddy don't get along."

The two women looked at me in surprise. The lady with the bob spoke first. "It happened so long ago," she said, "but I still remember because it surprised me so much. It's because Lily never RSVP'd to Geraldine's daughter's wedding. Geraldine was very offended."

The blue-haired lady woman gave her a funny look. She shook her head. "No, no, no," she said. "You have it all wrong. Lily was never invited to the wedding. She told me so. She was crushed. They were supposed to be best friends."

After they left, arguing over who had slighted whom, I stood there shaking my head. Aunt Lily was a stickler for manners. There was no way she wouldn't RSVP in a timely fashion to any invitation, especially one from a good friend. I realized what must have happened. Aunt Lily's invite had probably gotten lost in the mail. Two friends hadn't spoken in fifteen years, missed all that time in each other's lives over a simple misunderstanding. It was very sad.

Something had to be done. But unfortunately, I didn't have the time right then to figure it out.

Chapter Eleven

Happy Birthday to me, I thought as soon as I opened my eyes the next morning. I was officially a teenager, but I didn't feel any different. Not six inches taller or suddenly knowing how to apply eyeliner or anything like that. Just me, one day older.

I sat up in my bed. The heat wave had finally broken. As we had walked back from the store last night after finishing the centerpieces for the two parties, we had noticed a drop in temperature. We all opted to sleep in our own beds, and Mom and Dad seemed very relieved. No sleeping bodies to step over in the morning!

From the window by my bed, I felt a slight breeze coming in and I could hear the birds singing again. *Whew.* It was going to be a nice day for both parties, even if neither of them were for me.

After I brushed my teeth, I went downstairs. I heard someone bustling in the kitchen. I wondered if there would be a bouquet of delphinium by my breakfast plate, or if Mom had gotten up early to whip up special pancakes for me — maybe in the shape of a flower or something. Or maybe there would be balloons tied to my chair.

Wishful thinking.

Mom stood in front of the coffeemaker, frowning. "Where's your dad?" she said crankily. "I never know how to work this thing."

I stood there, waiting for her to turn around and wish me a happy birthday. But nothing.

My spirits sank. I couldn't believe it. I shuffled over to the fridge and peered inside forlornly.

"No time for breakfast," Mom said. "We have to get an early start. We'll pick up something at the Corner Café on the way in."

"Okay," I said. Maybe she needed a little reminder. "Do you think I should wear something special today?" I hinted.

Mom shook her head. "Dress down. We're going to have a very busy day."

We kept the store open for a couple of hours, then closed early to set up for the McGillicuddys' party. I was dragging my feet, feeling completely forgotten. Mom had never wished me a happy birthday. No texts or calls from any of my friends. And Hamilton . . . what I wouldn't have given for a birthday text from him. I had had some disappointing birthdays before, but this one took the cake.

As Mom and I loaded up the van with the centerpieces, Mom turned to me, holding an empty gilt frame. "Do we have the flower list?" she asked. She meant the page we had put together of the flowers the McGillicuddys had chosen and their meanings. I had printed several copies (better safe than sorry!) on thick ivory paper, which were still sitting on the worktable. I ran inside, picked two up, and placed them in a pink folder, which I put in my shoulder bag. The frame would be placed on a table set up at the entrance to the tent, along with some framed photos of the McGillicuddy family through the years and a mini version of the centerpiece.

When we got to the McGillicuddys', Mom and I rang the bell, each balancing a box of centerpieces in our arms.

There were several more in the car. Mrs. McGillicuddy came downstairs in a pretty pink dress and diamond earrings, a huge smile on her face.

"Welcome!" she said.

"You look marvelous!" Mom told her.

"Thank you," replied Mrs. McGillicuddy. "Didn't we luck out with the weather? What a gorgeous day!"

"Great day for a celebration," I muttered.

We walked through the entryway and out the back door to the backyard, where the tent was set up. I wanted to pause a moment to take a closer look at their beautiful garden, which prominently featured several different kinds of roses, all in full bloom. But there was no time. As the caterer bustled about and some of the grandchildren ran around in the backyard, we began setting up the centerpieces. Mrs. McGillicuddy hovered behind Mom as she displayed the family photos. She had a comment for each one. "That's our wedding day!" she said with a sigh. "And look at how cute Annemarie was as a baby!"

Mom finished arranging and took a step back. "It looks great," she said. She reached into a box and pulled out the gilt frame. "Now hand me the flower list," she said to me.

"Sure," I said, walking over to my bag and grabbing the folder. Then I had a sudden idea. It was last minute and a little crazy. Would it work? "Oh my gosh," I said. "I can't find it. I guess I forgot to take it."

Mom looked at me crossly and, in my current state of disappointment, it nearly brought tears to my eyes. "I *told* you to bring it. That's so unlike you." Mom shook her head. "I'll drive back and get it. But we're running out of time. We have to finish up here and shoot over to Society Sisters." She looked a little frazzled.

"It's okay, Mom," I said. "I'll take care of it." I grabbed my phone out of my pocket and began to walk to the front of the house.

"Ask Dad," she called after me.

But I had other plans. I flipped open my phone, took a deep breath, and crossed my fingers.

"Aunt Lily," I said when she picked up. "I need your help."

After we'd spoken, I hung up and took another deep

breath. It had taken some convincing, but Aunt Lily had finally agreed to help us out.

Twenty minutes later, there was a knock on the front door. I opened it to find my great-aunt, not looking too happy.

"Here you go," said Aunt Lily, handing me the flower list and immediately turning to walk back down the front steps.

"Lily!" said Mrs. McGillicuddy, sounding shocked. (I had told her moments before that I needed her in the front hallway.)

"I was just delivering something to my great-niece," Aunt Lily explained, looking embarrassed.

"Thank you," said Mrs. McGillicuddy stiffly.

I plunged right into it. "Look, I don't know how to bring this up, so I just will," I said, all in a rush. I was totally nervous this wouldn't work. "Mrs. McGillicuddy, you think Aunt Lily never RSVP'd to your daughter's wedding, and that's why you're mad. Aunt Lily, you never received an invitation to the wedding and you thought you weren't invited. And that's why *you're* upset." I looked at the two of them. "Don't you see? It was all just a stupid mistake. The invite must have gotten lost in the mail."

The two women stared at me, looking confused.

Aunt Lily shook her head slowly. "You're right. I didn't receive an invitation. For all these years, I thought you'd left me out."

Mrs. McGillicuddy blinked. "And all that time I thought you were incredibly rude," she said. Her expression softened. "I should have known you wouldn't forget to RSVP," she said. "You've always had impeccable manners."

Aunt Lily nodded, a rare smile stealing over her face. "And I should have realized my invitation was lost in the mail. We were so close. I was just too embarrassed to ask, so I assumed the worst."

"Will you forgive me?" they asked simultaneously, then burst into laughter. I couldn't help joining in. My heart felt lighter. My plan had worked

"Lily, today is a very special day for me," said Mrs. McGillicuddy softly. "I'd love if you could stay for our party."

Aunt Lily opened her mouth. I could tell she was about

to decline, but then changed her mind. "Thank you, Geraldine," she said, "I would love to."

I smiled at the two friends. Then I thought about Ashley and me. A lot of similarities and one big difference — Ashley had never invited me to her party, although I had saved it for her. *Not that I want to go anyway,* I reminded myself.

Mom walked into the entryway. "Del, did you get that list . . ." Then she noticed her aunt. "Why, hello there, Lily," she said.

"Hello, Daisy," said Aunt Lily. "I'm just catching up with my old friend, Geraldine."

I grabbed Mom's arm and we walked outside with the list, giving Aunt Lily and Mrs. McGillicuddy some privacy.

Mom looked at me funnily as we put the flower list into the frame and set it on the table. "I don't know how this happened, Del, but I assume you had something to do with it," she said.

I smiled. "I'll explain later," I told her. We finished setting up and headed inside to say good-bye to Mrs. McGillicuddy.

"Call my cell if you need anything," Mom told her. "Happy anniversary! I hope you have an amazing party."

"I've got it covered," said Aunt Lily. "Go to your next event." She gave me another surprising smile. "And thank you, Del."

"Anytime, Aunt Lily," I said. I couldn't help it. I had a really warm feeling inside. Del Bloom, friendship saver! Bringing old ladies together after years apart.

When Mom and I arrived at Society Sisters, we were pleased to see that the barn was almost totally decorated. We set to work lining up the luminarias, putting garlands of flowers on the tire swing, the benches, and the wooden fences. After the tables were set by the waitstaff, we started assembling the centerpieces. It was a bit complicated, but Mom and I soon got into a groove. When we were done, we surveyed our work.

"Amazing," we said at the same time. But Mom was looking antsy. "We're pretty much done here," she said. "But someone should stay till the grand reveal. Just to make sure everything goes as planned."

I nodded.

I wasn't prepared for what came next. "So . . . I hate to do this to you," Mom said, "but would you mind overseeing it by yourself? I'll be back in an hour or so to get you. I have some last-minute errands to run."

I stared at her in disbelief. "So you're leaving me in charge of my enemy's birthday party? All by myself. And on my . . ."

But Mom was already halfway to the van. "Good luck!" she called.

Was this really happening? Then I sighed. *In for a penny, in for a pound*, as Gramps always says.

Ashley and her mom arrived shortly afterward. I made sure the barn doors were closed tight so the surprise wouldn't be spoiled, and went to greet them.

I had to admit that Ashley looked, as usual, very glamourous in a strapless, pale blue silk dress with floaty layers. I thought of the simple sundress I had packed for my birthday dinner in Maine and smiled. Her hair was up in a French twist and she had on pretty, gold sling backs. She walked unsteadily down the path toward the barn.

It couldn't have been more perfect. The sky was turning a rosy pink and the luminarias glowed beautifully. The fairy lights danced in the breeze. The white-tuxedoed waitstaff bustled about, setting up the hors d'oeuvres tables. A handsome waiter presented the Edwardses each with a colorful drink in a champagne flute. "Watermelon sparklers," he murmured.

I felt a slight tinge of envy. But mostly I felt proud of the amazing last-minute party I had planned — which was about one hundred times better than the lame indoor party Ashley had planned for herself. Just saying.

"Open the doors," Ashley said. "I want to see the centerpieces." She gave me a look. "They had better be perfect," she added.

"They are," I replied confidently. "But you'll have to wait. We have a special surprise in store for you."

Mrs. Edwards and I exchanged glances.

Ashley looked like she wanted to argue, but then her guests began to arrive.

Mrs. Edwards touched my arm. "It's beautiful," she whispered. "Thank you so much, Del!" Then she added, "I hope the special surprise is a hit!"

As some of my classmates began to arrive, I decided it was time to fade into the woodwork. Though it would have been nice to talk to some kids I hadn't seen since the last day of school, I felt way too conspicuous in my dusty T-shirt, cut-offs, and Converse All-Stars. I especially had no desire to see Hamilton and his date. I slipped through the crowd with my head down, unnoticed.

"This is awesome!" I heard Carmine tell Penelope Peterson as he scarfed down a canapé.

"Totally gorge!" Rachel gushed to Samantha.

Just you wait, I thought.

I headed around to the back of the barn and went inside.

The room looked incredible. The luxurious chandeliers, decorations, Oriental rugs, and tables set with crystal and china, contrasted amazingly against the rough wood of the walls. The odor of hay mingled with the heady floral smell. And the centerpieces just blew me away.

The banquet manager strode over to me. "Everyone is waiting outside. Are we good to go?"

I nodded. "We're good to go."

A minute later, I threw open the barn door and stepped back into the shadows.

The guests at first just stared in amazement. Then they gasped. For the tables each had a centerpiece of tightly packed, deep red roses, studded with white stephanotis, which each had a sparkling crystal placed in the center. They looked like perfect shining stars against the field of red.

But what everyone was gasping about was the gorgeously glowing blue base of each arrangement. We had filled the large crystal vases with silica gel and added hot water. Once the gel had expanded, we layered in LED light cubes, then added the flowers. They were red, white, and blue, and totally breathtaking. Just like the Fourth of July fireworks that had inspired them.

Ashley stood there, her mouth open and her eyes wide. When everyone spontaneously burst into applause and cheers, she grinned widely.

I was close enough to see Olivia Post, our former Bridezilla, grab Ashley's arm and say, "Uh-ma-zing. I'm speechless."

My work here was done. I made my way incon-
spicuously to the back door. Or at least I thought I was
inconspicuous. Until I found my way blocked by the very
person I had been trying to avoid. You guessed it, Hamilton
Baldwin. Looking crazy handsome in a jacket and tie. The
same jacket and tie he had worn to the middle school
prom, I noted.

"Hey, Del," he said. "Nice centerpieces."

"Thanks," I said uncomfortably.

He smiled and waved someone over. My heart sank as
I realized that the person heading toward us was the girl
from Fleur. She was wearing a one-shouldered black dress
and high heels. I suddenly felt very young, very short, and
very underdressed.

"I'd like to introduce you to someone . . ." Hamilton
started to say.

My eyes widened in alarm.

"This is my . . ." he began.

"My mom's outside!" I blurted out. "I've got to go!"
And then, not looking back, I ran out the door.

I had just stepped outside when someone grabbed my
arm. I spun around, expecting to see Hamilton.

To my utter surprise, it was Ashley. "Del, I . . ." she started. "I . . . want to thank you for making my party so cool. For convincing me to have it."

"No problem," I said.

"I love it!" she said. She looked down at the ground. "I know it couldn't have been easy," she said. "Especially considering we're not exactly best buds anymore."

"I . . . uh . . ." I sputtered.

I watched in disbelief as Ashley pulled her hand out from behind her back and handed me a pretty frosted cupcake. "Happy Birthday, Del," she said, and disappeared back inside before I could say anything in return. Not that I would have been able to. I was completely and totally speechless.

Chapter Twelve

As I stood waiting in the dark parking lot, the sounds of laughter and cheers of Ashley's guests echoing across the parking lot, my excitement over the party's success was slowly overshadowed by other things. Disappointment that Hamilton had a girlfriend. Anger that the only person to wish me a happy birthday had been my worst enemy. I began to silently stew. I threw the cute cupcake into the bushes. Maybe the raccoons would enjoy it. I had lost my appetite.

Mom pulled up, the gravel crunching under her wheels. She had a big grin on her face. Wordlessly, I slipped into the passenger seat and buckled my seat belt.

"So?" she said impatiently.

"It was fine," I said. "She liked it."

I didn't say another word the whole way home.

Mom and I returned home to a dark house. I decided to try one last hint.

"It really was a special day," I said as we walked up the front steps, looking at Mom meaningfully.

"Mmmm-hmmm," she replied.

Shaking my head, I pushed open the front door and tripped over the shoes.

"Stupid Crocs!" I grumbled. I slipped out of my sneakers and headed upstairs.

"Del!" called Mom. "Nobody seems to be around and I need some help getting the fishing poles out of the back of the shed. Can you help me move the bikes?"

I rolled my eyes. Was she kidding? Of course I minded! Moving the bikes was a terrible, time-consuming job on any day! I took a deep breath and headed back down the stairs. Could this birthday get any worse?

I followed Mom out the back door into the backyard. I blinked. Were those lights hanging from the branches of our big oak tree?

Then I heard a chorus of voices call out: "Surprise!"

I blinked as I saw Dad, my sisters, and even Aunt Lily smiling at me.

Mom turned to me. "Happy Birthday, Del."

My eyes took in the paper lanterns; the white lights, the quilt thrown over the picnic table, the Mason jars filled with wildflowers, and the big jar with the spigot, filled with lemonade.

They remembered! I smiled at everyone in shock. Grateful, happy, shock.

I turned to Mom. "How in the world . . ."

"Becky," she said. "She called me from camp and told me about your dream party. I'm so sorry I had to leave you alone at Ashley's, but someone had to go pick up the lobsters."

"You mean we're having . . ."

"A backyard-kind-of-lobster bake," she said. "We have everything but the pit."

"I can't believe it," I said, blinking back tears. "This is amazing."

My sisters rushed over. "Happy birthday, dear Del!" they shouted, wrapping me in a big group hug.

Poppy started jumping up and down with excitement. "Del, you're never going to believe who's . . ."

And that's when Gran and Gramps stepped forward.

"Happy Birthday, Del!" they chorused.

For the second time that night, I was completely speechless. "I . . . uh . . ." My eyes went from Gran to Gramps and back again. They looked so tan and relaxed and happy. "I can't believe it!" I finally choked out. "I've missed you both so much! What are you two doing here?"

Gramps rushed forward to hug me, lifting me off the ground. "We couldn't miss your thirteenth birthday, now could we?"

After I'd hugged Gramps and Gran about ten times each, Dad led me over to the picnic table. As the paper lanterns swayed in the breeze, we started eating. First, we had New England clam chowder, creamy and delicious. Then came lobsters, corn on the cob, and lots of butter to dip it all in. After I had eaten every bite of lobster meat (nobody can eat a lobster the way I can), I squirted lemon juice on my hands to clean them off. (Wet naps are for wimps.)

After dinner it was time for presents. Turned out all of my friends *had* remembered and mailed me different gifts. I grinned as I opened them — a bottle of citrusy-smelling perfume from Heather, a pair of white plastic retro-looking sunglasses from Amy, and bizarrely enough, a pair of leg warmers from Jessica. She always buys the weirdest gifts.

I saved Becky's for last — it was a flat, rectangular gift wrapped in white paper with purple, curling ribbon cork-screwing across it. A book, for sure! I opened it up and stared at the familiar cover.

I laughed out loud. "*No Flying in the House!*" I cried. I flipped open the front cover and read what Becky had written inside:

Happy thirteenth birthday to my best friend, Del! Remember when we both read this over Christmas break in third grade and tried to kiss our elbows to prove we were fairies? I have a copy here at camp so we can read it at the same time again. I miss you!
XOX, Becky

I closed the book and hugged it to my chest.

"And this is from all of us," said Mom, handing me a slim box. I lifted the top and gasped as I saw what was inside — a tiny ruby pendant, my birthstone, hanging from a delicate gold chain.

"I picked it out!" Poppy boasted happily.

"I love it," I said.

Gran and Gramps had brought me a fun straw bag from Key West and a huge conch shell they had found and polished. Even Aunt Lily gave me a gift — a pretty jewelry box, where I could store my new necklace.

"Thank you for what you did earlier, Del," she said softly.

I felt embarrassed. "No problem, Aunt Lily," I said.

I looked at my family. My crazy, kooky, extremely generous, and thoughtful family. "Thanks, everyone," I said.

"Speech, speech!" Dad called out.

I gulped. I despise public speaking, even if it's just in front of my family. But I knew what I wanted to say. "You know," I began, "who needs a fancy catered party, anyway? This is shaping up to be the best birthday ever!"

"Hear! Hear!" shouted Gramps, and everyone clapped and cheered.

"Time for cake!" Poppy said. "Where is it?"

"It's coming," said Mom with a grin. I gave her a look. The cake was being delivered? Wasn't it a little late?

There was a knock at the back gate. Everyone just looked at me. "Go get it, Del," Mom encouraged me. Confused, I stood up, walked over, and opened up the gate. And there stood Hamilton Baldwin, holding a large, white bakery box. I just stared.

"You work for the bakery?" I asked, totally bewildered.

He laughed. "No, I don't."

Rose pushed up behind me. "Invite him in, Miss Manners!" she said.

I blinked and stepped back so he could come in.

"Wow!" he said, gazing around the backyard. "This looks great." He grinned. "Sorry I missed the lobster, but I had a" — he grinned — "prior engagement!"

I led Hamilton to the table and introduced him to my family.

"Hey, everyone," he said, as laid-back as ever.

"Pleased to meet you, young man," said my gramps, which made me laugh. Mom took the cake box from

Hamilton and then the rest of my family thoughtfully busied themselves getting plates and forks and knives.

I looked at him. "So . . ." I started.

"Becky called me," he explained. I grinned. When did Becky have time to play tennis with all the social arrangements she was making? I had to give my BFF a lot of credit.

"So I called your mom and asked her if there was anything I could bring. And she told me — dessert!"

I took a deep breath. "But what about your date?" I asked.

Hamilton looked confused. "My date?"

"The one you were about to introduce me to at Ashley's party!" I explained. Sheesh.

Hamilton looked like he wanted to laugh. "That wasn't my date. That was my cousin Melissa. She's here for the summer to help out my mom at Fleur." He smiled. "My mom makes me take Melissa everywhere with me since she doesn't know anyone." He smiled. "But now that she's settled in, I'm going to have more free time on my hands."

"Oh," I said, smiling. It all made sense. Why he blew me off. Why he and the girl had been in Fleur together. And why Ashley had said he was bringing a date to her party.

"So maybe when you get back from Maine, we could . . . go to the movies or something," Hamilton said, blushing a little.

"Definitely," I replied, my cheeks turning red, too.

From behind me, my family began to sing "Happy Birthday." I turned around. Mom was standing at the top of the steps holding a strawberry shortcake from Bella's!

I turned to Hamilton. "That's my favorite!" I told him.

He grinned. "Your mom told me. It's mine, too!" He looked at me. "Happy birthday to you, Delphinium Bloom."

A very happy birthday to me, indeed, I thought. *This evening just gets better and better.*

Mom placed the cake in front of me, glowing with fourteen candles, one for good luck. "Make a wish," she said.

Gran and Gramps were there. I was having the birthday party of my dreams (pretty much). With one very special guest. I wasn't quite sure what to wish for. I closed my eyes, thought of something, and blew out the candles, all in one breath.

"Hooray!" cried Poppy. "You get your wish!"

"Don't tell us what it is," Aster warned.

"And we have some special news," said Rose.

"Gran and Gramps are coming to Maine with us!" shrieked Poppy.

I gave Gran and Gramps each a huge hug. I couldn't have asked for a better birthday present.

I grinned at my family. They might not always do things exactly the way I hoped they would. But they had really come through for me today. It seemed like all my birthday wishes were being granted.

"And I'm coming, too!" added Aunt Lily.

"Yay!" I said weakly.

Okay, sometimes *all* your wishes can't come true!

Turn the page for a
sneak peek at the next
Petal Pushers book!

The house phone rang. I reached out a soapy hand and picked it up. "Bloom residence," I said.

"Hello, may I please speak to Daisy Bloom?" a woman's voice asked.

"May I ask who's calling?" I said, looking pointedly at my sisters, who were all lacking in phone etiquette skills. The twins simultaneously stuck out their tongues at me.

"This is Marlene Lewis," the voice said. "From the Homecoming Committee."

A big grin spread over my face. I held the phone to my chest and brought it to Mom, who was curled up on the living room couch knitting Aster a long black scarf.

"It's a woman named Marlene Lewis," I whispered. "She's from the Homecoming Committee."

Mom sat up straight and put her knitting to the side. I handed her the phone, then lingered in the entryway to listen.

"Hello, this is Daisy Bloom," she said. "Hi, Marlene, how are you? I can't wait to show you our amazing idea for the Homecoming bouquets. I was hoping we could set up an appointment this week. . . ." She paused to listen and a frown crossed her face. I leaned forward, worried. "Oh, I see. Is that your final decision?" Mom nodded. "Okay, well, thank you for your time. Good-bye."

I was too afraid to ask. Dad did it for me. "Oh, Daisy," he said sympathetically. "That didn't sound like it went so well."

Mom nodded grimly. "It certainly didn't. This Marlene person told me that she already hired another florist."

My heart sank. "Fleur," I said. I shook my head. I had been right to be suspicious at the mall!

Mom nodded grimly. "Fleur," she confirmed.

Dad frowned. "Marlene just started this fall. She probably doesn't know that Petal Pushers has always done the flowers for Homecoming. Do you think I should talk to her?"

Mom shook her head no emphatically. "She's allowed to make her own decisions," she said. But then she dropped her head into her hands. "But she didn't even give us a chance. This is the first time that our family isn't doing the Homecoming bouquets in seventy-five years. How am I going to tell Gran and Gramps?"

POISON APPLE BOOKS

The Dead End

This Totally Bites!

Miss Fortune

Now You See Me...

Midnight Howl

Her Evil Twin

THRILLING. BONE-CHILLING.
THESE BOOKS HAVE BITE!